THE CASE OF THE

UNEARTHED
EVIDENCE

THE CASE OF THE

UNEARTHED EVIDENCE

an Augusta McKee mystery

Susan Moore Jordan

ISBN: 978-1-950625-11-6

Published by Shaggy Dog Productions, LLC

Library of Congress Control Number: 2020918882

Cover design and art by Taylor Van Kooten

"Patrolman Donald Martin"
Contributed by Lieutenant Stephen R. Kramer (Retired)
Historian, Greater Cincinnati Police Museum

Books by Susan Moore Jordan

The *Carousel* Trilogy:
How I Grew Up
Eli's Heart
You Are My Song

Jamie's Children

The Cameron Saga:
Memories of Jake
Man with No Yesterdays

"More Fog, Please"
(non-fiction)

Augusta McKee Mysteries:
The Case of the Slain Soprano
The Case of the Disappearing Director
The Case of the Toxic Tenor
The Case of the Purloined Professor
The Case of the Chrysanthemum Murders
The Case of the Unearthed Evidence

Table of Contents

The murder of Patrolman Donald Martin
in March of 1961 was an actual case investigated by
the Homicide Squad
of the Cincinnati Police Department.
Det. Lt. Stephen R. Kramer (ret.)
made parts of his file on the case available
to the author for inclusion in this book.
Everything you read which is part of the factual
information about the case came from those files.

Prologue

October 22, 1918

It is done.

He leaned against the shovel for a moment, breathing heavily, wiping his sweaty forehead with a shaky hand. *I'll never have to see that face again.*

The wind had picked up and clouds now raced across the moon. He straightened, packed down the earth, smoothing it carefully until he could see no trace of what lay beneath.

Gravel, sand, and stones had been delivered a week earlier. The ground looked exactly as it should, ready to receive the flagstone patio which he would order completed the next day, obliterating forever what he had just done.

No, today. It must be after midnight.

The quiet in his neighborhood was shattered by the repeated sound of a gong—an ambulance racing down Madison Road.

No doubt another influenza victim. He shivered slightly. Cincinnati hospitals had been in crisis mode for nearly two weeks, overwhelmed by those needing immediate care. As an attending physician at General Hospital, he knew that sound far too well.

Four days was all they could spare me. Even for a grieving widower.

Emotions overwhelmed him—grief, rage, despair. He sank to the ground and clutched his head, feeling bile rise in his throat. *What have I done? Killed someone I once regarded as a friend.*

He dragged himself to his feet slowly, leaning heavily on the shovel. He felt he had aged twenty years during the past two hours. The wind grew colder and blew through the trees and shrubs around his house. The sounds of the rustling branches echoed the one word uttered by his victim before he fell to the floor: *Why?*

He glanced around the grounds one final time. No sign of the violence that had transpired. When the masons arrived, completing the work should go smoothly.

As he went inside to clean himself—*though the blood will never come off my hands*—he thought of his adored young son, safe with his aunt and uncle, far away from this city awash in plague and death.

Peter can never know.

Chapter 1
A Beyond Cold Case

Friday, October 22, 1965

"We feel sure we know who the shooter was. But the thing is, we have to be able to give the prosecutors proof so it will hold up in court."

Homicide Detective Malcolm Mitchell stabbed a bite of chicken Parmesan and rigatoni and stared at it gloomily.

"You know, one of the first things you told me about police work was exactly that," Augusta McKee responded to her husband. "I think you said 'It's one thing to know something, but it's quite another to prove it.'"

The Don Martin case had landed on Malcolm's desk for the second time since his fellow Cincinnati Police Department officer was killed four years earlier. Every detective on the force had worked on it at least once, and all were eager to find the proof needed to arrest the killer.

Augusta knew Mal found it frustrating and distressing. After four years, it was in danger of being considered a cold case.

"Here's what we know: three in the morning, a quiet night, and with his supervisor's permission Patrolman Martin was looking at cars in a lot on Reading Road."

"Yes, you told me about it. He and his wife were about to adopt a baby and decided they should buy a car."

"Four guys driving by witnessed the patrolman being shot and saw the gunman running away, and they stopped and went to Martin's aid. The first cop on the scene heard his last words: 'I've had it.' At first it was believed the killer had been a lowlife named Frank Murph—until it was determined Murph was in jail at the time of the shooting."

"And the theory is Martin was attacked by three men he found trying to steal a battery."

Mal nodded. "Two really bad guys, and one mainly just stupid. Brothers, Walter and Jesse Walls, and a friend, Charles Jillson, their getaway driver." He pointed at her with his fork. "I know you look for the good in people, Gus, but trust me on this one. Walter Walls is pure evil."

Augusta took a moment to consider her husband of six months, the most fascinating, attractive, remarkable, admirable person she had ever known. At the age of fifty-three she had fallen deeply in love. That Malcolm returned the love and they were now man and wife still amazed her.

"I would never doubt you, Detective. And the facts certainly seem to prove that—Walls shot Patrolman Martin with his own gun. Five times. Horrible."

He nodded. "The thing is, even though everything points to Walls as the shooter, we can't prove it. The witnesses arrived late, and they can't identify him. But all the evidence we've gathered indicates it had to be Walls. Every time he's been interrogated, he's claimed he didn't do it. Swears it. And his brother is terrified of him so he won't contradict him."

"What about the third man, Jillson?"

"Found dead in Kentucky. It's likely Walls killed him during one of the brief times he was out of jail. Jillson just drove off leaving the brothers without a getaway car. Walls has killed for a whole lot less. He's spent most of his adult life locked up somewhere."

"Surely his family knows something. Friends?"

"All terrified of him."

Augusta stood and took their plates and cutlery from the alcove, where they'd had an early dinner, into the kitchen. Malcolm followed and turned on the hot water as Augusta scraped the plates. Right behind them trotted the newest member of the McKee-Mitchell household, a six-month-old Golden Shepherd puppy, Fritz.

Mal grinned down at the pup, bent and scratched between his ears. "He needs a walk."

"I'll take him. I'll let these soak for a while. Why don't you stretch out for a few minutes? Maybe listen to some music." She picked up Fritz's leash as he wagged his tail furiously and whimpered in anticipation.

"Perhaps strategize about your next move with this stalled case."

"Thanks, Gus. And thanks for listening." He gazed at her warmly. Augusta drowned in his dark blue eyes, the first thing she had noticed when they met on the campus of Cliffside College.

That meeting had been confrontational. A student at Cliffside, one of two colleges where Augusta was a professor of music, was found dead in Emery Hall, the residence building on the campus, and Detective Malcolm Michell had denied Augusta admission. She made her way onto the campus through a path in the woods which required her to scale a four-foot stone wall, and Malcolm was dumbfounded when he saw her emerge from behind the greenhouse. But he allowed her to stay, eventually enlisted her assistance, and it soon became apparent something sparked between them.

Augusta had changed from her beloved stilettos into low-heeled shoes as soon as she arrived home earlier. She grabbed the jacket hanging on a hook by the back door and shrugged into it, then took Fritz down the walk which led off the grounds around her charming Tudor home and onto the sidewalk on Vista Circle. A turn to the left took them up a hill, and going around the circle made a walk of just over a mile, one she and Fritz took frequently.

Fritz, joyful as ever to be on an outing, trotted alongside Augusta as they enjoyed the crisp autumn air and, for Fritz, the smells of the neighborhood. But as they reached the home of the Worthingtons, three houses up the circle, suddenly Fritz bolted toward the house, pulling so hard on his leash that he nearly upended Augusta.

"Fritz! *Heel*!" Obedience school training had just begun, and "heel" was the current lesson. It was achieved with considerable effort on Augusta's part, taking several minutes to bring a determined Fritz under control. He finally acquiesced and they finished their walk without further incident.

But when they reached home, Augusta made the mistake of unclipping the leash from Fritz's collar before they entered the house. In a flash, he headed back toward the Worthingtons', his mistress following quickly, frantically calling to him. Malcolm heard the ruckus and watched in amusement as she chased Fritz out of sight.

"You're a big help," she remarked to a grinning Malcolm when she returned home and met him at the back door, out of breath and dragging Fritz behind her. "*Bad boy!*"

"Was that for Fritz or for me?" Mal laughed.

"Both of you."

"Could you tell what he was after?"

"He was furiously digging behind the Worthington's house." She knelt by the puppy. "What do you have in your mouth, Fritz?" She glanced up at Malcolm. "It looks like a bone or something, but it's covered in dirt."

He joined her and pried the item from the pup's mouth. "Let's see." Malcolm took the object to the garden faucet to rinse it off.

Augusta followed him to the faucet and handed the leash to him. "Wipe his paws before you take him inside. There's an old towel right inside the door."

"I know. Why don't I grab it and do that now?"

Augusta rinsed her hands and Malcolm wiped his dog's paws with the dampened towel. He picked up the item Fritz had dug from the Worthington's yard and examined it carefully.

"Gus…this isn't just any bone. If I'm not mistaken, it looks like a human heel bone."

Startled, she stared at him, feeling a chill run up her spine.

"Where did you say he was digging?" Mal again peered at the bone.

"In the Worthingtons' backyard. Among some loose flagstones, it looks like the patio is being replaced." She stared at him again as she realized what he had just said.

"A human bone, Mal? How is that possible?"

Malcolm's eyes narrowed and Augusta saw him move into what she considered "full detective mode."

"I have to talk to Charlie and Peggy. They need to know about this, and I need to look around that area." He peered at the sky. "And I have to do it now. It'll be dark soon."

Good Lord. Augusta's voice quivered as she spoke. "Are you suggesting there's more? That there's a body buried there?"

"I'm suggesting I need to take a look around. Stay here."

"Not on your life." Augusta shivered slightly as she hugged herself. "I'll put Fritz in the pantry with water and some chew toys."

At five feet nine, Augusta was nearly as tall as Mal's six feet one and matched him easily stride for stride. He gave her a sideways grin. "I like watching you run. It's kind of like watching a gazelle."

She had to laugh. "I wasn't running to entertain you. Having Fritz around has me in great shape, though."

"I'll say." A quick hug around her waist with one arm. "Let's hope this doesn't take too long."

Augusta and Malcolm had become friends with Charles and Margaret Worthington when the Worthingtons moved onto Vista Circle two years earlier. Charlie was a surgeon at General Hospital and Peggy a member of the Summer Opera Board of Directors. Augusta had known her for several years.

Mal rang the doorbell and Augusta wondered how on earth he would broach this subject to their friends. *Say, Charlie, I need to take a look at your patio. There may be a skeleton buried under there, old bean.*

Peggy opened the door and invited them in. "I need to talk to both of you," Malcolm said, wearing his detective face. "Can you come around to the back?"

Peg's demeanor changed. This was definitely Detective Mitchell speaking. "I'll get Charlie."

The four of them met behind the house, Charlie turning on the floodlights before he and Peggy exited the house through the sliding doors. "What's going on, Malcolm?"

"Hopefully nothing. But Fritz dug up an object back here just a few minutes ago. Charlie, first I need to hear from 'Doctor Worthington,' and if you confirm what I think this is, I need to be 'Detective Mitchell.'"

He handed the bone to Charlie, who recognized it immediately.

"My God. It's a heel bone!" He stared at Malcolm as Peggy gripped his arm.

"I thought so. We need to see if there could possibly be anything else back here."

The two women stood to one side as Charlie went back into the house, then returned with two strong work lights. Staring at the area which was now flooded with artificial light, the men zeroed in on one particular spot which seemed slightly darker than the rest.

"I'll get a broom." Charlie once again disappeared for a moment into his house, returning to brush away dirt, gravel, and sand, being careful not to step into the darker area. After only five minutes of clearing, another bone was revealed, a large one. Charlie, who had begun to perspire, turned to Malcolm. "Holy Christ, that's a femur."

Charlie walked away from the area and sat down heavily on a lawn chair. "It has to have been here for years. Who knows how long ago the patio was installed?"

"So it would appear," Malcolm responded. "Obviously, a crime was either committed here, or the body was deposited after this individual died in another location. We're probably looking at a decades-old burial site."

"What do we need to do, Malcolm?" Peggy's voice trembled.

"I'm sorry to say this, but this is now a crime scene, and I need to make some phone calls. I have to call my boss, and he may or may not assign me to this case. I also need to get in touch with the coroner. Then I can tell you what happens next."

Peggy stepped forward. "Come inside, Mal. You can use the phone here."

The two of them went inside and Augusta moved closer to her neighbor. "Fritz dug up the heel bone?" Charlie looked up at her.

"Maybe a half-hour ago. He got away from me. Sorry."

"I'm not. Much better to find this tonight than to have the masons come in tomorrow and quite possibly destroy the bones. Who was this?" He leaned forward and ran a hand through his hair. "I'll tell you, Augusta, this is pretty unsettling."

"Oh, I'm sure it is," she replied. "Do you have any idea when the patio was installed?"

"Not a clue, though the condition suggests it was long ago. We learned from the previous owner that the house was built in 1910 by a surgeon at General Hospital, Thomas Reichenbach. We're actually the fourth family to live here." He gave her a sideways glance. "And to think, we've had a tenant we never knew about."

Augusta had to laugh. "Oh, Charlie. This is definitely creepy."

He sighed. "Maybe too creepy for Peg. She may not want to stay here tonight. Once the bones are gone, I think she'll be okay."

"You're welcome to stay with us," Augusta offered. "I'm not sure how much sleep I'll get. I imagine Malcolm will be here while the coroner and his team are working, anyway."

"That's generous, Augusta. We might take you up on that."

Peggy and Malcolm returned to the patio. "The coroner is contacting his team and they should be here in about an hour. My partner is on his way—we are assigned—and so are a couple of uniformed officers. No lights, no siren. I have no idea how long this will take, but I'm afraid they'll be digging up your yard for a day or two, starting tonight. I'm sorry."

Peggy moved to her husband, who stood and put his arms around her.

"Mal invited us to stay with you tonight, Augusta," she said.

"Great minds think alike." Augusta smiled at Peggy. "I just made the same suggestion to Charlie."

"Thank you. I'll get a few things. And quit apologizing, Detective. I want this done as soon as possible. I'd really like to get away from here as soon as I can. Charlie can stay if he wants, but I have absolutely no desire to watch a team dig up a skeleton from my backyard." Peggy shivered and laughed a little shrilly.

"Then you and I can go back to my house, Peg." Augusta would have liked to watch what the coroner and his team did, but she felt it the better choice to be a good

22

neighbor. Peggy was definitely on edge and Mal would tell her what was found.

By the time Peggy packed an overnight bag and rejoined them outside, a car pulled up and Gary Ridgeway, the Hamilton County coroner, stepped out. Augusta knew him as a pleasant man and a capable organist who used to play at the Episcopal Church in Hyde Park. He still substituted there on occasion, and Augusta had been guest soloist at that church more than once when he accompanied her.

Even though Gary was at the Worthingtons' home in an official capacity, his manner was calm and reassuring. Before becoming coroner, he had been a funeral director with a highly successful practice. The idea of working also as a crime solver appealed to him immensely and he had gone back to school before running for office.

He greeted her pleasantly. "Well, Augusta. I understand your dog found this intriguing case for me?"

"So it seems, Gary. Quite by accident. Who would ever think to find a skeleton under a patio in Hyde Park?"

"Who indeed?" He turned to Malcolm. "My team is on its way."

Peggy grabbed Augusta's arm. "Which means I'd really like to get out of here, please."

"Yes, of course." The two women turned and started walking down the hill.

Oh, I'd so love to see how they do this. Two more cars drove up the hill as they entered Augusta's house. *It seems this skeleton was a person who died long ago. And it's quite possible he or she was murdered.* A shiver ran up her spine.

Talk about a cold case.

Chapter 2
Neighbors and a Friend

"I remember the dog you had here last year for a few months." Peggy Worthington, comfortably ensconced on the sofa in Augusta's large living room, took a sip of her wine. "He was a German Shepherd and Golden Retriever mix too, wasn't he? Beautiful animal."

"Caruso. Yes, he was. He belongs to a young officer on the CPD, Trevor Davidson, and we took him in when Trevor was severely wounded during a drug raid."

Peggy stared at her. "You know, we live in such a bubble here in this area. We don't often think about our police putting their lives on the line for us at times."

"All the time, Peggy. They're not supermen, but it takes a special person to be a good law enforcement officer. Fortunately, Trevor is completely recovered—and back at work. He loves what he does."

Peggy nodded. "What is it again—'protect and serve'?"

"Absolutely." Augusta scratched her puppy's head. "You'll love this: Fritz is from a litter Caruso sired. We named our dog after another great tenor, Fritz Wunderlich."

Fritz dropped his chin on his paws and gazed at his mistress soulfully.

"I've heard of Wunderlich," Peggy chuckled. "Do you ever call him by his full name?"

"Oh, it happens. When he does puppy stuff." She patted her knee and Fritz moved to curl up at her feet. "Look, he thinks I'm reprimanding him. You're a good boy, Fritz." She scratched his head.

"He's a lovely animal. How old is he?"

"Six months, so he's probably about three-fourths of the size he'll be when he's an adult dog." Augusta laughed. "It's a good thing he's not full sized yet, he's already a handful when I walk him. That's why we've started obedience school."

"My grandkids will want to meet him when they're here for Thanksgiving."

"I'm sure he'd love that. This breed is very child-friendly."

Fritz looked from one woman to the other, sitting up and perking up his ears, as if he realized they were talking about him. "Lie down, Fritz," Augusta ordered, and Fritz obediently sank to the floor, chin on his paws, again gazing up at his mistress.

Peggy glanced around the room. Augusta kept the sliding French doors between living and dining rooms open, so it was one large, unbroken space. The sofa and several inviting chairs, occasional tables, a stereo, and a cabinet for recordings filled the living area. A Baldwin concert grand took up much of the dining area, though there was a dropleaf table against the far wall. In addition, a smaller serving table stood near the door to the dining alcove. Glass French doors opened from the alcove with its wide bow window into the dining room. The entire downstairs had a spacious, airy feeling. Augusta had decorated primarily in greens and blues, with softly patterned oriental rugs.

"I'm impressed this room doesn't reflect that a dog lives here," Peggy remarked.

"We're careful not to let him in this part of the house unless someone is home. And we make sure he has plenty of chew toys."

"That explains why I don't see teeth marks on the table legs," Peggy laughed. She took a final sip of her wine.

"Oh, there've been a few. Mrs. Bluefield and I have become experts with one particular brand of furniture polish." Augusta lifted the bottle of cabernet sauvignon and looked at her guest.

"Yes, one more would be fine." Peggy glanced at her wristwatch. "How much longer do you think they'll be?"

"I have no idea, but they could be quite late. If you'd like to turn in, that's fine."

Peggy sat back, kicking off her shoes. "I'm not sleepy. What a thing to have happened. Finding a body—well, the remains of one—in my backyard."

"Hardly an everyday occurrence."

Peggy's eyes fell on framed photos of Malcolm's sons, Ryan and Dan, on the fireplace mantle. "Let's talk about something more pleasant. How was Danny's wedding? I haven't seen you since."

"It was beautiful. Danny and Martha are so happy. They just returned from their honeymoon in Hawaii."

"Our Andrea and Kevin went there for their honeymoon. Six years ago. They loved it." The Worthingtons had two children and now a total of six grandchildren. Peggy had commented when they moved into the house on Vista Circle that it was too much house for just the two of them, but their children and grandchildren were frequent guests.

"What about Martha's career? Has she made any decisions?" Martha Van Camp had been Augusta's student when she first met Dan, Malcolm's younger son, a year earlier. A very fine soprano, she had been determined to attempt a career as an opera singer and still had opportunities she was exploring.

"Not yet. She has an engagement with the Louisville Opera Company in the spring and is seriously thinking about entering the Met Opera Auditions as well."

Dan was a patrolman on the Cincinnati Police Department, with aspirations to follow in his father's footsteps and eventually become a detective. He had a degree from the University of Cincinnati in Criminal Justice and had joined the force two years earlier.

"Another diva and detective story in the making," Peggy commented.

Augusta laughed. "Maybe. Danny is very supportive of Martha and has encouraged her to even accept opportunities in Europe if they come along. She's afraid if she does that, she'll miss him too much during the time they'd have to be apart."

"I suppose time will tell." Peggy yawned, covering her mouth with the back of her hand. "Oh, sorry. I guess I am sleepy. I'll excuse myself. You're so kind to invite us to stay here while my backyard—I guess I should say, the crime scene—is dug up."

Augusta carried their stemmed glasses into the kitchen, washed them, and put them away. *Two o'clock.* She took Fritz outside, shivering as she waited while he sniffed around for a few moments. He followed her back into the living room, Augusta curling up on the sofa with the puppy lying on the floor beside her.

Another crime right here in my neighborhood. How my life has changed since I met Malcolm. Only a little over a year earlier, Augusta had experienced the most frightening time of her life—abducted and held captive by a mob boss in a house only a short distance away. Caruso had helped find her, and Mal had saved her life.

I used to think the final dress rehearsal for an opera or musical theater production was the height of excitement. Little did I know. Augusta smiled, remembering her first encounter with her dark-haired, handsome detective and the many times since when she'd found herself in a dangerous situation far removed from musical drama.

She sat up as she heard Mal and Charlie talking quietly as they came into the house. Mal gave Charlie directions to the guest room before heading for the kitchen.

"I'm not asleep."

"Let me grab something to drink."

He rejoined her, beer in hand, and sank on the end of the sofa. Fritz stood at his knee, tail wagging. "They've called it a night. Two uniforms are on duty guarding the premises." Mal ruffled the fur on the dog's head.

"How far did they get?"

"The bones are pretty much cleared of debris. Some of the smaller ones are degraded, but most are in surprisingly good condition. Gary's team laid a protective covering over the skeleton to keep him—it—safe."

"The victim was a man?"

"Well, Gary said it appeared to be, but he wants to be sure before he commits to anything official about our bones." Mal took a swallow of beer. "Gary is one amazing guy. Talk about working patiently. One of the people on his team took about a hundred pictures. They'll take more photos in the morning, and then finish brushing soil off the bones before they take them to the crime lab. I imagine that will take most of the day." Mal finished his beer, stretched, and yawned.

"Did they find anything else besides the—remains?"

"They haven't really looked yet. Once the bones are safely removed, we'll go over the entire site carefully. I think if I killed a guy and buried him, I'd be inclined to throw the murder weapon into the grave as well."

He stood, pulled her to her feet, and glanced over his shoulder at the pup. "C'mon, Fritz. Let's call it a night."

***

Augusta rose early, made coffee, and laid out breakfast choices for her guests: fruit, cereal, bread for toasting, scones she'd fortunately picked up at Cincinnati's historic Findlay Market only two days earlier. Mal had grabbed coffee and a scone before heading back to the Worthington house, and Charlie and Peggy appeared just as he was leaving.

"This is lovely, Augusta." Peggy placed figs, grapefruit sections and a kumquat on a small plate, and added an orange scone. "I hate to be a nuisance, but I'm not ready to go back to the house yet. I'd like to wait until the investigation into the crime scene has been completed and I can contact the masons to come back and install the new patio."

"You're not a nuisance, Peggy. I do have to go to the Conservatory for a short time, I have office—well, studio hours on some Saturday mornings. Mostly for make-up lessons."

"I'll be fine. I can take Fritz for a walk if that's okay." She stared into her coffee cup. "We'll head in a different direction, though. Not past my house."

"That would be great, he'll love it. We're working on 'heel' if you don't mind trying that with him."

Charlie finished his breakfast and carried his dishes into the kitchen. "Many thanks, Augusta. I'm going to drop off my stuff at the house before I head to the hospital. Hopefully, by the time I get home the coroner's team will have completed their work."

"In which case, I'll head home as well," Peggy remarked. "Even if Malcolm's team is still working, I think I'll be okay with that. I just want the bones gone."

***

A tap on her studio door and Millicent Devereaux, Augusta's closest friend, popped her head in. "Do you have any appointments?"

Milly, a compact, energetic woman with bouncy salt and pepper curls, had earned her reputation as an exceptional pianist and much-sought-after teacher. She and Augusta were students at the Conservatory during the early thirties and had spent three years together in Europe after their graduation. Augusta would be eternally grateful to her friend for helping her through the trauma of losing her first love to pneumonia when he was only twenty. Though the women had been separated by distance during the ensuing years, they had never ceased being best friends, and Milly returning to Cincinnati a few years ago to join the Conservatory faculty struck Augusta as the friendship coming full circle.

"No one scheduled anything. I thought I'd stick around until noon or so just in case."

Milly settled comfortably in a chair near Augusta's desk. "Okay, tell all. What the hell is going on in your neighborhood now?"

Augusta stared at her. "How in the world did you find out? Oh, wait. Garrett. He's like a magnet for that kind of news." Milly's steady beau, Garrett Stoddard, was a well-known criminal defense attorney.

"He's fascinated. Skeletal remains in your neighbor's backyard? Of indeterminate age?"

"Well, it isn't known exactly how old at this point. But yes, they were buried under a flagstone patio behind the house. Masons had been separating and removing the stones in preparation for replacing it. Did you hear how we got involved? Fritz dug up what proved to be a heelbone."

"Like father, like son," Milly chuckled. "First Caruso tracks you down and helps free you from Nunzio Ponti a year ago. And now Fritz has uncovered a cold case."

"You know, I never thought of that. Canine detectives at work."

"They could start an agency—'The Doggy Detective Duo'." Both women laughed.

"Peggy Worthington is freaking out. She and Charlie stayed at our house last night, but she says once the coroner has taken the bones to the lab she'll go back home. Charlie is okay, though he did make a remark about having an 'unknown tenant' in his backyard. It's definitely creepy."

"Garrett was told Malcolm and Jim were assigned to the case. Where do you even start? Do they know when the patio was built?"

"Not really. The house was constructed in 1910 by a Dr. Thomas Reichenbach, so the patio can't be any older than that. And it may well have been added at a later date. I suppose that it should be easy to learn from building permit records."

Milly leaned forward. "Dr. Reichenbach? I know who that is. He retired some time ago; I think not long after World War II. He died fairly recently—maybe in 1959 or1960. There's a son, Peter, who teaches German at U.C. He's also quite a good pianist."

Augusta's eyes widened. "I'm acquainted with Peter Reichenbach. And come to think of it, I met Dr. Reichenbach once, somewhere. Oh, I remember, at a fundraiser for CPD Police Academy scholarships. Interesting. I never connected the two men, and I didn't even think of it last night. Peter is a really nice guy. I guess he'll be notified—and maybe questioned."

"Probably. But I don't think Thomas Reichenbach was living in the house on Vista Circle when he died. In fact, I recall Peter telling me his family moved out to Indian Hill in the twenties."

"Charlie said he and Peggy are the fourth owners of the house. They only moved in a couple of years ago." Augusta shook her head. "How do you know all this stuff?"

"I'm a nosy broad and I know a lot of people," Milly quipped. "By the way, I'm sure you didn't get much sleep, but you look great. No red in those hazel eyes. My friend Augusta, the woman who never ages."

"It's all those walks with Fritz."

"Partly. It's also your great hair colorist Jason who keeps that becoming light chestnut shade just right. I'm sure the stilettos spend a lot of time in the closet these days."

"You're right about that," Augusta laughed. "I have a whole new wardrobe of low-heeled walking shoes. And Caruso taught me to keep those stilettos far out of doggy reach."

Milly observed her friend appreciatively. "I like that dress. Coral is a good color for you. Someday you must tell me what it's like to wear an A-line dress." She glanced down at her own ample bosom. "Something I could never pull off."

Augusta laughed. "Milly, you have a lovely, womanly figure. While the current styles happen to suit my shape better, styles change all the time. Who knows what will be popular next?"

"Yes, who determines that? One of life's little mysteries, I guess." Milly grew serious. "Speaking of mysteries, you're embroiled in another one. I swear they just look for you. You don't have to do a thing."

"That's not quite true. I fell in love with a homicide detective. And my life became a whole lot more interesting."

"Interesting—or complicated?" Milly arched an eyebrow.

"Both. Maybe 'fascinating' is a better description." Augusta smiled. "All I know is, I wouldn't change a thing."

Chapter 3
When Does a Case
Become a Cold Case?

Gary Ridgeway's team had removed the bones from the Worthington's backyard by late Saturday afternoon, allowing Peggy and Charlie to return home, where Mal and his crew had just started their scrutiny of the ground. At about nine o'clock Mal and Jim agreed to keep a security detail on hand overnight and return the next morning to complete their investigation.

Augusta had food waiting for Malcolm when he came in the door. "I need a shower first, Gus. That smells great, though."

While she waited for Mal to come back downstairs, Augusta took Fritz outside for a bit so she wouldn't be interrupted as she heard exactly how the coroner's team handled removing bones from a shallow grave. Mal reappeared fairly quickly, dressed comfortably in sweats and heavy wool socks.

"Man, I'm beat. I'd never make it as an archaeologist. All that crawling around on the ground. Major muscle cramps." He helped himself to meatloaf, mashed potatoes, and a vegetable mix, piling his plate high.

"Well, tell all," Augusta leaned forward eagerly. "I would have loved to have observed at least a little of this. I have some idea of how painstakingly archaeologists remove artifacts from soil. So this was similar?"

"Gary enlisted my aid since he was short-staffed. Gus, I swear some of those brushes he used had about three hairs. They tried to remove every speck of dirt off every one of those bones." Mal took a long swig from the beer Augusta had set out for him. "They took dozens more photos. They must have hundreds by now."

"It does sound very much like an archaeological dig."

"Well…in a way, it is. I asked Gary if he could tell anything about how long the victim had been there. He said there were so many variables he really wouldn't venture a guess until he had the bones back at his lab and could clean them up better."

Mal ate steadily for a few minutes. "Archaeological dig for sure. That was one high-powered team at work. A couple of forensic scientists and an anthropologist from the University. I was in awe of those people. They even took some soil samples from different areas to check the pH balance. Like I said…talk about *thorough*."

"Did they find anything else in the grave?"

Mal took a hearty bite of meatloaf and potatoes at the same moment she asked her question, so she waited patiently until he swallowed. "A couple of important items. A sharp knife of some kind. Possibly the murder weapon."

"And?"

"And a pocket watch. The kind my grandfather gave my dad. Gold. Maybe with initials. Gary showed it to me but it was so dirty it was difficult to tell. But an expensive watch, I believe."

"Anything else?"

"A few shreds of fabric. Maybe wool. Some broken pieces of buttons."

"All possible evidence, I would think."

"Yes, you think correctly. We'll go over the area again in the morning, but I believe eagle-eye Gary got everything."

"After you've finished, do you plan on smoothing out the ground for the Worthingtons' masons?"

"Yes, certainly. We'll take our time looking, though, before we do that."

"Will you be there all day tomorrow?" Augusta placed another slice of meatloaf on Malcolm's plate.

"Probably not the entire day. My guys are coming back at eight. We may be finished by noon." He looked at her quizzically. "Why, do we have plans or something?"

"No plans. I was hoping we might have a little 'us' time, though."

He grinned broadly. "I think that can be arranged. In fact, that's kind of what I had in mind after I finish eating."

"I thought you were beat," she laughed.

"Just got my second wind." Mal leveled his irresistible blue eyes at Augusta and drained his beer.

***

On Monday, Jim Edmonds made a visit to the Hamilton County Courthouse to find paperwork on the house Thomas Reichenbach had built. The Auditor's Office provided the history of ownership of the house, and the Recorder's Office had details on physical changes that had been made. Jim also stopped at the Cincinnati Public Library to find any stories that might have been written about previous owners.

He shared his findings with Mal at Detective Headquarters later that morning.

"Dr. Reichenbach applied for a permit to have a patio installed in October of 1918. The house was sold in the spring of 1921 to Donald Davidson, and again in 1952 to Anthony and Elizabeth Bartlett. Your friends bought it in September 1963 and their permit to replace the patio is on file as of last month."

"No other building permits for additions, garage, or anything of that nature?"

"Garage, added in 1925 by Davidson. Also, the house was rewired and replumbed in 1945 when Davidson owned it, and the kitchen was redone in 1952. I would guess after the Bartletts moved in."

"Will you see if you can contact either of those previous owners and confirm the patio wasn't replaced at some point? Those bones seem awfully well-preserved to have been in the ground for close to fifty years."

"Sure, I'll see if I can find them. Davidson may not be around, but I'll bet I can locate Anthony and Elizabeth—the lady who wanted a shiny new kitchen."

Jim turned to leave but had another thought. "Have you been in touch with Peter Reichenbach yet? He needs to be told about this."

"He will be. I'm hoping Gary can come up with some idea about who the victim might be, though that's probably a long shot. I'm waiting to hear from him."

"Roger that."

Knowing he most likely wouldn't hear from Gary Ridgeway for several days, Mal put what he'd begun to think of as "the Mr. X case" on the back burner. Instead, he opened the Don Martin file, reviewing some of the details of the crime.

On the night of March 10, 1961, Patrolman Martin was working the night shift and requested permission of his supervisor, Sergeant Hike Bogosian, if the radio traffic was quiet, to check out the downtown Lincoln Mercury car lot on his beat at 715 Reading Road. Sergeant Bogosian approved his request and, at 3 a.m., Patrolman Martin radioed Communications that he would be on foot in the area. He parked his patrol car at the National Biscuit Company (Nabisco) parking lot at 721 Reading Road, exited his vehicle, and walked onto the car lot.

Over time, the homicide detectives—including Mal—who worked the case put together additional facts: *We know Walt and Jesse Walls walked to a nearby bar because neither of them had a drivable car. We know Walt called his friend "Cadillac Charlie" Jillson for a ride, and the three of them went looking for a battery to steal. Unfortunately, we believe they headed for the same car lot Patrolman Martin would arrive at not long after they did.*

The next section of the report was part conjecture and part evidence from eyewitnesses who arrived late at the scene, too far away to identify the shooter or his accomplice.

Patrolman Martin approached the two at the front end of a car with its hood open. A violent struggle ensued. Walter Walls, possibly with Jesse's assistance, gained control of Patrolman Martin's Smith & Wesson Model 10 .38 Special service revolver and shot Patrolman Martin in the chest.

Patrolman Martin turned and ran toward his patrol car with Walter Walls in pursuit, shooting him twice more in the back. Patrolman Martin slumped to the ground, held his hands up, and Walls took deliberate aim and fired another round into his back.

Mal refilled his coffee mug and went to a window, leaned against it and watched traffic moving smoothly along Eighth Street. *I'm Don Martin. I go into this car lot, hear voices maybe, and then see two guys standing at the front of a car. It's three in the morning so they're obviously up to no good. I'm a cop, it's my job to try to stop what could be a theft in progress. Do I go back to my car? No, petty thieves. I can handle this.*

Malcolm frowned. *But Don made mistakes. He didn't have his stick with him, and his uniform blouse is buttoned. With a cross-draw holster he can't quickly get to his gun. Still, he moves to them. 'Police! Stand still and put your hands on the car.' Then it all goes to hell.*

Now he's in a fight for his life. They're all trying to get the gun. Buttons are popping off. His collar is ripped in the fight. Cross-draw holster—the asshole has a better chance of pulling it out than he does. Walls gets the gun and as he pulls it out it's pointed at Don's chest, and he feels the shock the instant he hears the gun go off. Don was a medic. He knows he's in trouble, but he's seen guys survive chest wounds. He's got no gun. All he can do is run.

At 3:10 a.m., Charles Minnich, Jack Wenner, Hugh Moore, and Harold Stiver, all of Phillipsburg, Ohio, were northbound at 721 Reading Road when they observed the chase and fourth shot. After Patrolman Martin fell to the ground, Walls walked up and fired a fifth shot into his head behind his left ear.

Observing the scuffle and homicide, Jillson drove away.

Mal tried to take another swig of coffee but his throat closed up. *God. What would it have been like, hearing two shots from his own gun that hit him in the back? He must have been in unimaginable pain. Struggling to breathe. 'Negotiate. It's my only chance.' He stops…puts his hands up according to the kids. Walls takes aim and shoots again. Then walks up and puts one into his head. Hard to believe Don was still alive, but Max says he was when he got there.*

That fifth shot behind his ear—something the press never knew about. Mal clenched his jaw. *He had to know he wasn't going to survive. I can't imagine his thoughts.*

He returned to his desk to scan the final section of the report. The four men from Phillipsburg then saw Walls shoot at Jillson's car as he drove away. The shooter, Walter Walls, was last seen running across Reading Road and up a muddy embankment, while Jesse ran in a different direction. When the crime scene was first investigated, the gun and muddy clothing were found stuffed into a trash can. One of the witnesses, Harold Stiver, tried to give Martin aid while the other men drove to a gas station and called the police.

I need to go back to the scene of the crime and walk through it again, Mal mused. *Walt Walls has been questioned more than once. He continues to deny he killed Martin, even though at one point while he was in prison again after that, he bragged about killing a cop. And no way in hell is Jesse going to give him up.*

The phone on the desk buzzed. "Mitchell."

"Detective, your wife is here. She asked if you could see her."

A nice diversion. "Sure, Griffith. Send her in."

He stood just as Augusta poked her head around the door. "Do you have a few minutes?"

Mal put his arms around her and kissed her briefly. "Just going over the details of the Martin case for about the hundredth time," he sighed. "What's up?"

"Can I take you to lunch? I have some information about your other case that might be helpful."

Seated in the same bar where they had shared their first lunch more than two years earlier, she gazed at her husband as she leaned on her elbows. "I don't think I mentioned to you that I know Dr. Thomas Reichenbach's son, Peter. He teaches German at the University of Cincinnati, and he's also an amateur musician. A pianist."

"No, you hadn't told me that." He took a bite of his burger. "I need to contact him soon. Probably tomorrow."

"Here's something else. The Worthingtons remembered they have a history of the house. It includes a paper indicating that the patio was built in October of 1918. Peggy told me about it when I was walking Fritz this morning."

"Yes, Jim got that info from the city's records."

"Mal…October of 1918 was the period when the Spanish influenza was at its worst in Cincinnati. I spent some time at the public library this morning. From what I read in newspapers from the era, the county and city governments were in total chaos. It seemed nobody could decide who was in control. There were daily changes in decisions that were made."

"Go on."

"Ask yourself this—why would anybody decide to build a patio at that time? Not only that, but the last two weeks of October were the worst. All of the hospitals were overwhelmed. Things actually didn't get better until January. I read in one account that Dr. Reichenbach was at General Hospital, and he must have been there almost non-stop. It just seems very odd."

Mal stared at her thoughtfully. "What made you think about the Spanish flu?"

"My mother died of the flu that same year. That same month. I was eight years old."

"Good Lord, Gus." He rested a sympathetic hand on her arm. "That must have been devastating."

"Well, I think I've blocked most of it. As soon as she got sick my dad sent me to the Poconos to stay with my grandparents. My Uncle Lenny, my mother's younger brother, came to Philadelphia to collect me. He was only twenty at the time. I've told you about him." She smiled. "A brilliant world traveler who is also the man who taught me to use a shotgun to knock down clay pigeons."

Mal grinned. "Yes, I'd like to see that. You've told me he's still living in the Pocono Mountains."

"My grandparents had a beautiful summer home in a community called Buck Hill. The houses were called summer cottages, but they were large, spacious, and anything but cottage-like. Many of the homeowners were Quakers from Philadelphia; my grandparents were not. Lenny still lives in that house."

Mal finished his coffee and nodded to the waitress who appeared quickly and refilled it for him. "You know, I never heard my folks talk about the Spanish flu. The flood of 1937, I heard a lot about that. The First World War. Cincinnati's king of bootleggers, George Remus. And all the bad mob activity across the river during that same time. But I don't recall ever hearing anything about the flu."

Augusta nodded. "I stayed in the Poconos for months. My dad came up after my mother died. When we returned to Philadelphia, we moved into a new house." She finished her grilled cheese and tomato sandwich and dabbed her lips with her napkin. "You're right, people just didn't talk about it. Back in Philadelphia I was in a new school, taking music and dance lessons, making new friends. I missed my mother, but my dad saw to it I stayed busy. We visited her grave sometimes. Mainly people were happy World War I was over. Life went on."

She gazed into her coffee cup. "Seems odd, doesn't it? I know a lot of people died. But I guess everybody was focused on the war. So many American boys went to fight. But Malcolm, ten times as many Americans died from the epidemic than died in combat."

"We talk about the 'Spanish flu.' I guess that's where it started?"

"Actually, it didn't. It's believed the flu started here in the United States, and our military took it across the Atlantic. Because of the war most journalists didn't report on the epidemic even when it spread to Europe. The only country not involved in the war was Spain, so those reporters were free to cover it. Hence the 'Spanish flu' appellation. Classic case of 'shooting the messenger.'"

Mal pushed his chair back. "Well, I should get back to Headquarters and see if I can think of some way to close the Don Martin Case. I sure would like to solve this for Henry Sandman. Sandman's partner was killed six months after Henry became Chief of Detectives. And five years later Martin—who was his secretary Gail's husband—was killed. Sandman's got his twenty-five years in, and there are rumors he's pulling the plug."

"You mean he's retiring."

"Yes. And I'm afraid my boss is ready to pull the plug on this case. It's been over four years."

"Does that mean it will become a cold case?"

He nodded, stood, and held her chair for her.

"I'm sorry, Mal. You've got a couple of tough ones on your plate right now."

"What you said about the timing of Reichenbach having the patio built," Mal helped Augusta on with her coat. "It almost sounds as if he might have planned to murder the guy we found and had it worked out that the body would disappear."

"So, you think the good doctor could be the killer?"

"At the moment, he's the most likely suspect, yes." He paused. "No. He's the only suspect."

Chapter 4
Peter Reichenbach

Tuesday, October 26
8:00 a.m.

"Located both of them. Davidson's living with his daughter in Western Hills, and the Bartletts have a homey little three-acre spread in Indian Hill." Jim helped himself to coffee.

"Let me guess," Mal said. "They both say they didn't replace the patio."

"You got it. I was right about Mrs. Bartlett, by the way. You should see the kitchen in her new manse. Definitely a kitchen lady." Both men chuckled.

"Okay, we'll go with their word for now. Next step, contact Peter Reichenbach and let him know what we've uncovered. He was ten years old in 1918. This is a new one for me. How do you tell a man there's a chance his late father—a well-respected doctor—may have buried a body behind the house he grew up in?"

"You don't tell him that," Jim said. "You tell him your dog dug up a bone behind the house he grew up in and it seems it came from a skeleton that was…oh, cripes." Jim ran a hand over his dark crew cut. "How *do* you tell him about this?"

"Yeah. We'll have to think about this one. At this point, we have absolutely no idea what happened back all those years ago."

"We want to see if he can identify the items we found along with the remains. Are those in the coroner's Crime Lab?"

"Yes, but I think Gary will permit us to use his Property Room to show them to Dr. Reichenbach."

"Doctor?"

"His *curriculum vitae* says he has a Ph.D. in German Studies."

Jim grinned. "I had two years of Spanish in high school. The kids who took German looked down their noses at us Spanish students."

"Spanish was my language in high school, too. And now I have a wife who can speak German and is fluent in French. Talk about intimidating."

"I guess," Jim laughed.

Mal stood and pulled on his sports jacket. "I'm headed over to the Crime Lab to see where Gary is with our bones. I'll ask if we can invite Peter Reichenbach to take a look at the objects he discovered. Can you call the University and find out which building Peter's office is in and what his schedule is for today?"

Jim picked up the phone. "Roger that."

On arriving at the lab Malcolm saw that the coroner had the bones now arranged on an examining table as they would have appeared in the body. Mal had been impressed with the methodical, deliberate packing of each item as it was removed. The bones also looked clean, with no speck of dirt.

"Looks like you gave Mr. X a bath."

Gary laughed. "I guess you could say that. As I had surmised, he was a male, so your appellation of Mr. X is correct. I need him to start talking to me, and he had to be cleaned up better to do that."

"What has he told you so far?" Mal, intrigued, drew closer to the table, wondering what in particular Gary was looking for.

"So far, only that he was an adult male. He had a compound fracture of his left tibia that never healed quite correctly, so he very possibly walked with a limp. Maybe used a cane."

"Has he told you who killed him? How? And why?"

"You're asking him quite a bit, Detective Mitchell. Means and motive. What about opportunity?"

"It's pretty obvious to me that the killer created his own opportunity. Especially since the knife is most likely the murder weapon."

"It very well could be. Strong and sharp enough. Eventually Mr. X will tell me all of these things—except motive." Gary picked up a caliper, eager to get back to work.

"Well, I'll leave you two gentlemen alone. I know you'll be in touch as soon as you have something."

"Never fear. It will be a while, though." Gary turned back to his examination.

***

"Here we are," Jim said, as they reached the door to Peter Reichenbach's office in stately McMicken Hall. Before they could knock, Reichenbach appeared, papers and books piled precariously in his arms. As always, Mal did a quick assessment: *Medium build, average height, thinning brown hair, glasses.*

"May I help you?" Peter Reichenbach looked at the two men quizzically.

His balancing act with the books concerned Jim, who stretched out his hands. "May I help *you*, Dr. Reichenbach?"

Peter chuckled and allowed Jim to remove the loose papers he was close to dropping.

"Thanks. I don't usually do this, but I was running late for the class I just taught and forgot my briefcase."

"I'm Detective Edmonds. This is Detective Mitchell."

The expression on Reichenbach's face grew more puzzled. "Detectives? From the CPD?"

"Yes, sir," Malcolm confirmed. "May we speak with you for a few minutes?"

Reichenbach unlocked the door to his office and ushered them into a pleasantly cluttered room, the walls lined with bookcases, photos of his wife and children on the desk.

"Please, sit down, gentlemen." Motioning them to a small sofa, he relieved Jim of the papers he'd been holding and leaned against the front of the desk. "What's this about? I don't think I have any unpaid parking tickets."

"No, sir." Malcom leaned forward. "We need to talk to you about the house you used to live in on Vista Circle in Hyde Park. There's been an unusual discovery in the backyard."

"What—a body?" Reichenbach chuckled.

Neither detective responded. They continued to stare at him steadily for a moment that grew longer and longer. Mal watched the blood drain from Reichenbach's face.

"A body?" he repeated faintly, the seriousness of the situation beginning to sink in. He moved behind the desk and sat down slowly.

"The remains of a body," Mal told him. "We have reason to believe it might have been buried there in October, 1918."

"Good God. I haven't been in that house since…since 1921. My father sold it and we moved to Indian Hill."

"Yes, sir. We are aware the house was sold to a Donald Davidson that year, and it's changed hands twice more in the past forty-four years. The current owner received a permit to replace the patio. The bones were discovered last weekend."

"Under the patio?" Reichenbach nervously stacked papers on his desk, his hands shaking slightly. "Good Lord. I played there all the time." He pulled a handkerchief from his jacket pocket and mopped perspiration from his face.

"This is a lot to take in. Can you tell me anything else?"

Mal nodded. "The remains have been removed and are now at the coroner's crime lab, where they are being examined to determine whatever can be discovered about who the person was." He carefully avoided using the word *victim*.

"There were a couple of other items found with the remains," Jim said. "And we would appreciate your coming with us to the crime lab to see if you recognize either of them."

Peter Reichenbach sat back and blew out a breath. "I can't believe it. How did it—the remains—get there? You say buried under the patio?"

"You're the only person who lived in the house at that time who is available to us. I imagine memories from that long ago might not come easily, sir." Mal said.

"Well, Detective—Mitchell, correct?" Mal nodded.

"You must know that 1918 was a difficult year for this entire country. First of all, there was the war. The Great War. The war to end all wars. That sure didn't happen, did it?"

"No, it did not," Mal said. "I fought in the South Pacific in the next one."

"You were a Marine, then, or Navy? I was Army, but assigned here in the States."

"Marines."

Jim chimed in. "Marines, too. Korea was my war. Two tours."

They sat for a moment, three military veterans appreciating their common bond. Peter sighed. "And now Vietnam. It never ends, does it?" He shook his head.

He continued, "Back to 1918. Then there was the worldwide pandemic. The so-called 'Spanish flu' that killed so many of our countrymen, including my mother."

"My wife Augusta's mother died that fall as well," Malcolm remarked.

Reichenbach gazed at him. "Is that Augusta McKee?"

Mal nodded.

"Of course. Sorry, Detective Mitchell. I should have made the connection. You were married last spring, I believe. And solved that international case with the Chrysanthemum Quartet members not long after. I knew Saul Kronenberg and Michael Robinson. What a shock."

"And now I'm investigating another, Dr. Reichenbach. Unfortunate circumstances."

"Peter, please. Well, this seems unreal." He gazed from one man to the other. "Of course, I'll look at anything you need me to, and I'll try to remember whatever I can. I'm not sure how much help I'll be, though. That was a long time ago, and I was very young."

Jim stood. "Do you have time now? The Crime Lab isn't far."

"No, it isn't. One of my colleagues in the science department has been working on a case there. Maybe *this* case. And yes, I don't have another class until late this afternoon, so this works well."

***

Augusta waited in the Conservatory's Recital Hall for her private student Fernando Diaz, a bass-baritone with great promise now working toward his graduate degree. He had been cast as Death in Gustav Holst's opera, *Savitri,* which she was directing. They needed to deal with a staging challenge for the opera, scheduled to be performed the following weekend. Augusta had no lessons for the day; all of her students were involved in a Cincinnati Symphony Orchestra concert for the coming weekend, a performance of Beethoven's Ninth Symphony, and they were scheduled for rehearsals all day.

I'd love to get a look at those bones.

As a high school student, Augusta's intense interest in history had caused her to consider briefly attempting to become an archaeologist. Her science teacher advised her as kindly as possible there really wasn't much of a chance she'd be out on actual digs, but more likely would become a museum curator. While that assessment of the field had been true back in the mid-twenties, she was happy to see it was now changing to more digging opportunities for women. But she knew her eventual decision to pursue music was the right one.

Still, it would have been fascinating to be part of a dig. Now there was one in her own neighborhood and she hadn't been able to watch. *There has to be some way I can get into Gary's crime lab and see those bones.*

Fernando joined her in the Hall. "What's your thought, Professor McKee? It's pretty daunting to have to start this opera singing a cappella and try to capture the audience's attention."

"Here's what I hope to do. We're going to have a scrim pretty far downstage because the action primarily only involves the three leading characters. We'll have a backlight far upstage, and if you stand close to it, you'll throw a large shadow against the scrim."

"Wow. That's an attention-grabber for sure."

"It certainly should be," Augusta laughed. "My main concern is this, I'd like your voice to fill the auditorium as much as possible, especially when you sing the words 'I am Death.'"

"So, what you want me to do this morning is stand all the way at the back of the stage and sing that a bunch of times while you walk around the auditorium, right?"

"I knew you were a smart young man. Yes, please."

For the next fifteen minutes, they worked on this. Augusta wanted to avoid using a microphone, and she was sure Nando's voice had grown in weight and size and it shouldn't be necessary. She moved to different areas in the room, positioned herself and raised a hand, and he continued singing the first few words of the opera until she was satisfied.

"Bravo, Nando. You've passed the test. The audience will be constantly aware you are Death." Fernando smiled his appreciation of his heightened presence on stage.

Other singers had begun to arrive for the ten o'clock concert rehearsal and Augusta left the room, stopping occasionally to speak with a student. She knew they were to rehearse until noon, take a lunch break and then report to Music Hall to rehearse with the symphony at two p.m.

She drove to Peggy Worthington's and picked up the envelope Peggy wanted her to give to Malcolm, the information about the patio installation in 1918 by Dr. Reichenbach.

Maybe I can somehow parlay this into a chance to get into Gary's lab.

Augusta stopped at her house to make a phone call and take Fritz outside. Since she knew she'd only be out for a short time, she hadn't confined Fritz to the pantry. *He's been doing so well recently.*

Unfortunately, the minute she went inside, she saw Fritz the Good had been overcome by Fritz Wunderlich the Bad. Feathers everywhere, and a badly chewed throw pillow—her favorite—in shreds. Fritz happily trotted up to her, tail wagging, tongue lolling from his mouth.

Augusta picked up the destroyed remains of the pillow and shook it in his face. "*Fritz Wunderlich Mitchell, you bad dog!*" She dragged him into the pantry and closed the gate—the third they had installed, this one extra-strong. He slunk into a corner and gazed up at her sorrowfully. "Don't give me those puppy eyes. You were a *bad boy!*"

Well, it's a good thing I have a little extra time. Calm down, Augusta. He's a puppy. Vacuuming up feathers was annoying, but she got most of them. She checked her watch and called Detective Headquarters to learn that Malcolm and Jim had gone to the University to talk with Peter Reichenbach, intending to take him to the coroner's office if possible.

Augusta put her coat on and picked up Fritz's leash, returning to the pantry and unlocking the gate. He eyed her warily. "Oh, come on, bad Fritz. You need a walk."

He moved toward her slowly, head down, tail wagging only slightly. She laughed, bent down and laid her face against his neck. "I know you're sorry. Just don't do it again."

Actually, this works out well. I should get to the morgue right about the time Malcolm and Jim will be there, hopefully with Peter.

Chapter 5
Memories of the Past

Mal, Jim, and Peter Reichenbach waited in Gary's office after arriving at the coroner's building on Eden Avenue. A CPD Detective, Buck Grimes, was assigned permanently to the coroner's office, and he brought the two items from the Property Room for Peter to view. Each was in a sealed envelope with several signatures, that of each person who had handled them. Buck removed them and placed them on the table in front of Peter.

"Is it okay if I pick them up?" Peter asked Malcolm.

"Yes. Detective Grimes will re-seal the envelope and indicate who handled it, date and time. But be careful. There's still fingerprint powder on them."

Peter picked up the knife gingerly and held it away from himself. "I'm not fond of knives. I don't really know how my father did what he did."

The three detectives looked at each other, sure that Peter hadn't realized what he'd just implied.

"You mean being a surgeon," Jim suggested.

"Yes. I never had any desire to pursue that kind of a career." He continued to examine the knife. "Well, I've seen knives similar to this one, but I can't say I remember seeing this knife specifically."

He turned his attention to the pocket watch, picking it up and holding it for a few moments. "You know…this reminds me of something…something about my childhood. A watch like this one. My dad's best friend had one, and he let me hold it whenever he came to our house." Peter turned the watch over. "But his had his initials on it. I remember that. There aren't any on this one." He handed the watch to Buck, who repeated the process of resealing the envelope and amending the record.

Initials that could have been degraded over all these decades. Malcolm thought. "Who was he? Your father's best friend?"

"Wesley Vandergriff. He was a classical organist apparently on track for a major career. He was scheduled to make his debut in Europe that next spring. Sad that it never happened, because he was another victim of the 1918 flu." Peter turned to Mal. "Vandergriff was well known in musical circles back in those days, and organists still mention him from time to time."

Buck picked up the phone as he was preparing to return the items to the Property Room. "Yes, he's here." The men glanced at him and he motioned to Malcolm. "Your co-detective."

Jim grinned as Mal, annoyed, took the phone. "Yes, Augusta?"

Much to Malcolm's growing irritation, Jim and Buck continued to listen to his end of the conversation, while Peter seemed lost in thought. "Yes, we can do that. —Fine. Please make it quick."

He hung up the phone. "Augusta has some information the Worthingtons asked her to get to me and she's just outside." He glared at Jim. "I guess you told HQ we were on our way here."

"She's calling from a pay phone? This must be vital information," Jim remarked, stifling another grin.

"No, probably not. It's Augusta dying to see what Gary's doing with the—" He stopped, not sure how to put it.

Peter said helpfully, "—the bones? The skeletal remains?" He grinned wryly. "You don't have to tiptoe around the words on my account, Detective."

Mal stared at Peter. "I think I should tell you. We live on Vista Circle. Augusta was walking our dog, Fritz, when he dug up one of the bones Friday night and that's what led to the discovery of the remains."

To his surprise, Peter burst out laughing. "Augusta has a reputation for being—shall we say—assertive, Detective Mitchell. And usually to good purpose."

"I apologize. It was unfortunate that she showed up while you're here."

"Not at all. This happened a very long time ago. Right now, it seems like some kind of—well, fictional story." He gave them a crooked grin. "Maybe a true Grimms' Fairy Tale?"

All three detectives chuckled.

He's handling this incredibly well, thought Malcolm. *I like this guy.*

Peter continued, "Maybe if I could see the bones, it will be more real."

***

Augusta tapped a little nervously at the door to the coroner's office. She'd heard the comment Buck made, referring to her as Mal's "co-detective." *Oh, I'll bet he hates that. Which is probably why Buck said it; he has a wicked sense of humor.*

Buck grinned as he opened the door for her. An unsmiling Malcolm lifted an eyebrow, which confirmed he was annoyed. She turned her attention instead to Peter, who stood as she entered.

"Peter, I'm so sorry about all this. I have to take some responsibility." She handed Malcolm the envelope she was carrying.

"Yes, Detective Mitchell tells me your dog did some sleuthing. I guess it just runs in the family," Peter chuckled.

My word, he's handling this surprisingly well, Augusta thought. "Still, it can't have been easy to learn about the—" she stopped.

Peter laughed. "Augusta, we've already been through this. You can say 'bones' or 'skeleton' or 'skeletal remains.' They are what they are."

"Still, it must have been a shock to learn about them…it."

"Definitely, and I have no clue as to why they were there. I doubt I'll be much help. I was only ten in 1918 and thirteen when we moved away from that house. That was a very long time ago, and in a way, I'm finding it a fascinating story that I'm peripherally part of."

"Detective Mitchell tells us you're interested in seeing the remains, Augusta," Buck said. "It turns out Dr. Reichenbach is as well. I'll see if Gary has a few minutes."

Augusta glanced at Mal again, who was frowning as he studied the papers she had given him. "There is one interesting piece of information here, Augusta." He handed the items to Jim.

"Oh, good. Can you tell me what?"

"The name of the mason who built the patio in 1918. The company may still be in business. There could be more information in their records."

Jim looked up from perusing the file. "I'm surprised that information wasn't included in the county records. But that was over forty years ago, and as Dr. Reichenbach has reminded us, it was a turbulent time not just here, but worldwide."

"Peter, please, Detective Edmonds. Or—Jim, If I may."

Jim grinned. "Absolutely."

Buck stepped back into the room. "Gary's taking a break, and he's available to talk to you for a few minutes."

Augusta managed to pull Malcolm aside for a moment. "Are we okay?" she asked softly.

"We'll talk about it later. But yes, we are."

Seeing the skeleton laid out so carefully on an examining table surprised Augusta. *I don't know what I expected. But it looks so…clinical.* Staring at the bones, she tried to imagine how this person might have appeared in life. *Tall. Long fingers. It's difficult to try to imagine a face on his skull, though there are forensic artists who can do that.*

After introductions, Peter studied the skeleton. "So, this is the guy I was bouncing a ball on top of all those years ago." He glanced at Gary. "Or is—was—it a woman?"

Gary looked over his glasses at Peter. "No, it's the skeleton of a male, that much I can say with certainty because of the configuration of the pelvis."

"I have to tell you, Dr. Ridgeway, this is pretty surreal." Peter stared again at the bones.

"No doubt. Detective Mitchell was here earlier, and I haven't made much progress answering the questions he had then. It takes time. Forensic anthropology is a very exacting science."

Gary glanced around the room, and saw he had everyone's undivided attention. "Eventually, we will be able to give you the approximate age of our friend here— Mal calls him 'Mr. X'. We may also be able to ascertain exactly how he died."

He pointed to the skeleton. "As you can see, the bones are laid out here exactly as they were when Mr. X was a living human. That's the first step—we can see immediately if there are any bones missing. You'll see some of the small bones were degraded and a few were not found. Fingers and toes, mainly."

"Is that unusual?" Jim asked.

"No, not at all. The indications are this body was buried in 1918. Actually, most of the bones are in surprisingly good shape. Most likely because of the composition of the ground under the patio slab—the sand and gravel foundation. And a favorable pH balance in the soil. Some bones have been found in decent shape after hundreds of years, while others can disappear in a decade."

He glanced at his listeners again, and continued: "To ascertain whether Mr. X was killed deliberately—or even accidentally—we look most closely at bones in the areas of the head, neck, rib cage, and groin for knife or bullet marks, since most mortal wounds are located there. It's very difficult to kill a man with a knife or gun without nicking a bone or two."

He looked around again as if to see if anyone had a question. "As I said, this takes time. I doubt I'll have an official report for Detectives Edmonds and Mitchell before sometime early next week."

"Thank you, Gary." Buck's comment indicated it was time for them to let the coroner resume his work.

"Not at all. Oh, Dr. Reichenbach, I'm impressed that you wanted to see the remains."

"Well, it makes it a little less surreal. It's still hard to wrap my mind around what happened all those years ago, though. And why."

They were quiet as they filed from the room, absorbing what they'd just witnessed. Mal paused to speak privately to Gary before he joined them in the hallway.

"We'll drive you back to the campus, Peter," Jim offered.

"I can do that," Augusta said immediately. "I'd like to. It will give Peter and me a chance to talk."

"I'd like that. Thanks, Augusta," Peter responded.

Mal frowned. "Don't you have lessons this afternoon?"

"Not today. All of my students have a special rehearsal this afternoon for the Cincinnati Symphony concert this weekend. Beethoven's Ninth Symphony, remember?" She smiled sweetly, slipping her arm through Peter's.

***

"Do you have time for lunch?" Augusta eased her 1963 sapphire blue Chrysler Imperial into traffic, headed toward the U.C. campus.

"Yes, I do." He glanced at his watch. "My next class is at three. Only it's my treat."

"We're not far from the Vernon Manor Hotel. Their coffee shop is usually quiet and the food is good. How does that sound?"

"Ideal."

Seated in the pleasant room, orders placed, Augusta gazed at Peter. "It must have been a shock to learn about the discovery of human remains in the backyard of the home where you grew up."

"That's a pretty accurate description. It took a while for it to sink in. Now I'm beginning to wonder what happened. Why were they there?"

He glanced around the room, appreciating the soft colors in the décor, damask drapes at the windows, and the glow from the fireplace. "It's nice here. I don't think I ever knew about this place."

"I've enjoyed this coffee shop since my student years at the Conservatory." Augusta took a sip of her tea.

"You know, you and I have something in common besides music and students learning to speak and sing in German."

"Oh?"

"Detective Mitchell mentioned that your mother died of Spanish flu in 1918. My mother—Alice Reichenbach—also died that fall. In fact, in October of that year."

"In my case, as soon as my mother got sick my dad contacted my uncle in the Pocono Mountains and asked him to come and take me out of Philadelphia. The disease was very bad there."

Peter nodded. "My grandparents took me out of Cincinnati to stay with my aunt and uncle in Kentucky before my mother became ill. My father wanted us both to go, but she didn't want to leave him alone."

"Neither of us were able to attend our mothers' funerals, then. How strange it was to be away from home for several months, and then return to a house where there was no mother present—ever again. My father never remarried."

The server came with their meals and Peter waited until she moved away before replying. "Nor did mine. And after a couple of years he decided to sell the house. Her death altered him. Oh, I don't mean he wasn't a good father. But he seemed different. For one thing…he didn't like to talk about her."

"My father talked about my mother almost constantly. As though he couldn't accept that she was really gone." She gazed at him thoughtfully. "I don't know which might have been worse."

"I don't either. We did have pictures. One was a portrait that hung over the fireplace in the living room. I still have it. He put fresh flowers near it every week, even during the winter. So even though he didn't want to talk about her, he acknowledged her existence, in a way."

"I know your father sold the house on Vista Circle in 1921. Where did you move to?"

"Indian Hill. Lots of acreage, and I loved living there. In fact, my family is still in that house. I think you've met Mary Ellen. And you know my son Pete attended the Conservatory as a piano major."

Augusta nodded. "Yes, I remember him being there. He attended Juilliard for graduate school, right? And now he's teaching at the New England Conservatory. Quite an accomplishment."

"You know, though," Peter took a drink of coffee. "I think it was a great disappointment to my dad that neither his only son nor only grandson went into medicine. Neither of us had any desire to do that. And, truth be told, I was thrilled when Pete opted to study music. I enjoy what I do, but sometimes I wish I'd had the courage to tell my father what I loved most was music."

"You're a very good pianist, Peter. And don't you substitute on organ at the Church of the Redeemer in Hyde Park from time to time?"

"Well, I try. I don't consider myself an organist by a long shot." Peter sighed. "I just wish I had more time to practice. These days I have a pretty heavy teaching schedule, what with my classes at U.C. and at Xavier and Mt. St. Joseph."

Augusta raised her eyebrows. "I don't know how you juggle three schools. Two is all I could possibly handle."

"Ah, but you do more than teach, Augusta. You direct stage productions as well. I'll bet your schedule is busier than mine." They laughed together.

Peter grew thoughtful and gazed into his coffee cup. "This thing about the body in the backyard. I've been trying to make light of it. But there are some…well, in a way, it's troubling. How did it happen to be buried there? Who could have done it, buried a body and then obviously covered up that act by building a patio on top of the grave?"

"That's what the police are attempting to find out."

"When you think about it, there are only two answers. Either the masons did it…or my father did. I don't even like to think about the second possibility."

"I can understand that."

He leaned toward her. "And who is the man who was buried there? While I was at the coroner's office, I was shown two items that were recovered from the grave. A knife—which I guess might have been used to kill the man—and a pocket watch."

71

"Mal told me those items were found."

"I keep thinking about the pocket watch. It was like one a close friend of my father's owned. He came to our house frequently, and he would let me play with it. Gold, only his had his initials on it. W.V. I remember the elaborate etched letters and flourishes."

"W.V.?"

"Wesley Vandergriff. Maybe you've heard of him? He was a professional classical organist who toured throughout this country and Canada." He paused. "Another victim of the Spanish flu. He died not long after my mother did. He didn't have any family, so my dad had to take care of all the arrangements. Poor Dad. First, he loses his wife to that awful disease, then his best friend. No wonder he never liked to talk about that period in his life."

"I've heard of Wesley Vandergriff. He was highly regarded back in his time. The organ teachers at the Conservatory often say they wish they had heard him. One of them has some re-mastered recordings he made. I didn't realize he died during the flu pandemic, though."

"A lot of people died. Almost seven hundred thousand in this country alone. Probably millions worldwide."

"It was epic." Augusta folded her napkin across her plate. "It's been suggested that it was so awful, once it was over, people just wanted to forget it. So over time, it seems that's what has happened. Kind of a 'collective amnesia' about that entire experience."

She dropped Peter off at McMicken Hall and headed home. *I would guess he's going to wonder more about what his father might have done that resulted in the body we discovered.*

It's certainly possible he's the one who murdered Mr. X. But why?

Chapter 6
Another Way to View Life

Mal stopped at Mecklenburg's Beer Garden for schnitzel and German fried potatoes. Far too much food for Augusta after her large lunch; she put half her meal in the refrigerator for Mal if he wanted a snack later.

He seemed out of sorts, and she was sure she knew why. "I know you aren't happy with me showing up at the coroner's office today, but I did want to get that information to you from Peggy Worthington."

"Sometimes you go too far, Augusta. That could have waited." He frowned as he stabbed a bite of schnitzel.

"You're right, of course."

"Frankly, I'm more annoyed that you commandeered Reichenbach for lunch. Jim and I missed out on a valuable opportunity to speak with him further about his father's possible—probable—involvement in what most likely was a murder."

She stared at her plate for a moment. "Obviously, I didn't think. Really, all he said about that was that he didn't like to think about it. He said he could see two possibilities as to how the remains were buried in his backyard—either the masons did it or his father."

"Anything else?"

"Mostly we talked about our mothers, and how our fathers reacted to the sudden death of their wives." She repeated to Mal what Peter had said. "And we talked about his love of music, and his son Peter Junior's musical accomplishments. I knew young Peter when he was a student at the Conservatory."

"Did he say anything about a man named Wesley Vandergriff?"

"Yes, he did. Vandergriff was his father's best friend. He told me you showed him a gold watch that was very much like one Vandergriff let him play with as a child. He also told me Vandergriff died of the flu not long after his mother did, and his father made all the arrangements for his burial since his friend had no family."

Augusta noted Mal's eyes narrow on hearing this information.

"So that's important?" she asked.

"It could be. Keep this under your hat, but I asked Gary to recheck the watch for any vestiges of initials. Where was Vandergriff buried?"

"That he didn't tell me, but I'm sure you could easily find out."

Malcolm nodded and his expression softened. Augusta decided she'd been forgiven.

"I am sorry, Mal. But how fascinating to see what Gary is doing with our bones."

He had to laugh. "Oh, they're 'our' bones now, are they?"

"Well…Fritz and I did see them first. Or at least one of them."

It was a pleasant late fall evening when she left Mal and Fritz playing fetch in the fading light as she drove to the Conservatory for an opera rehearsal. Speaking of her mother brought many memories to mind, but they were more of her father trying to keep those memories alive for her.

It is strange how little I remember about my mother's death. And about my mother. Augusta turned onto Madison Road. *I remember how pretty she was. Or do I really? I've seen many pictures. I still see Lenny from time to time, and they had a strong resemblance. It's apparent in old pictures.*

Life and death. Mal's determination to close the case on Don Martin's murder. A skeleton buried apparently quite deliberately many years ago under a patio the same year her mother died. *Eileen Paynter McKee died at the age of thirty. She was so young.*

As she neared the Conservatory, Augusta turned her thoughts to the opera. When John Edmanston, the director of the opera program at the Conservatory, asked her to direct Gustav Holst's chamber opera *Savitri* for their fall workshop program, she readily agreed. Augusta knew nothing about the work other than its name and that she admired the composer. She appreciated the music of all the Victorian era British composers: Holst, Elgar,

Vaughan Williams. The music she had heard from them showed strong influence of English folk music.

Reading the background of the story made Augusta aware why this music was so different from Holst's earlier work. The fact that it was based on a section from an ancient Sanskrit poem, the *Mahabharata*, she found more than a little daunting.

She found a recording to listen to, conducted by the composer's daughter. The opening of the opera Augusta thought riveting: offstage, a cappella, the voice of the bass singing Death:

Savitri! Savitri! I am Death.
I am the law that no man breaketh.
I am he who leadeth men onward.
I am the road that each must travel.
I am the gate that opens for all.

This is so powerful, she thought. From the first time she heard it, Augusta considered Nando Diaz a strong candidate for the role.

Directing this opera challenged her, and Augusta felt she needed the challenge. Her knowledge of Hindu lore being limited, she decided to talk with her friend Dennis Halloran, a young Jesuit priest on the faculty of Cliffside College. They had been on a first-name basis since Dennis' student years at Xavier University, and he became her tech director for all the musicals she directed at Cliffside. Dennis had earned three degrees and Augusta believed her brilliant friend knew at least a little something about everything. Hopefully, he would be able to give her some insight into the story of this opera.

Augusta's one day on the Cliffside campus was Wednesday. She had lessons in the morning and a Music Literature class in the afternoon, followed by more lessons. As usual she and Dennis met for lunch, enjoying the chance to spend time together. As they were leaving the dining hall, she surprised him. "May I set up a time to see you later?"

"You want to make an appointment with me?" Dennis asked. "We could just talk now."

"No, this is serious business. May I come to your office at say, four o'clock?"

"That will work. You won't give me any idea what this is about?"

"See you later."

At four o'clock, seated next to his desk, she said, "Oh wise Jesuit priest, explain Hinduism to me."

Dennis grinned. "The long or the short version? It's simple and complicated at the same time."

"The version this lady can understand to help her direct an opera. Gustav Holst's *Savitri*. I've been studying the text for about a week, and I have some faint glimmer of what it's about. The operative word there is 'faint.'"

Augusta had the score with her and opened it. "There are three characters in this opera: the wife, whose name is Savitri, the husband, Satyavan, and the third character is Death."

"I've heard of the opera. Quite a departure for Holst from his early works."

"Why does that not surprise me? I mean, that you've heard of the opera." She tapped a finger on the score. "Holst seems to be deep into Eastern mysticism with this one. For instance—let's start with the word *maya.*"

"*Maya* is the theory that all of life as we mortals know it is an illusion. Only God—Brahman—is reality. Each soul is immortal and has been here forever, constantly evolving. There's a lot more—many rules and a whole pantheon of gods and goddesses."

"Well, I believe we have one of those gods in the opera. Death appears and tells Savitri that he has come for her husband. But that's actually an illusion as well?"

Dennis chuckled. "As I said, simple but complicated."

"Satyavan, the husband…the tenor…drops down dead after about the first ten minutes of music. Oh, by the way, it's a short opera. Only a half hour. Anyway, Savitri manages to persuade Death to give her a boon. He tells her she can ask for anything *except* the return of Satyavan. He has to go through the gate of death with Death."

"Let me guess. Savitri outsmarts him."

"Exactly. Death agrees to give her life, but she wins her husband's return when she persuades Death she has no life without Satyavan. This is getting pretty convoluted."

Dennis laughed heartily. "I can provide more detail about Hindu beliefs if it would help."

"No, I asked for the Reader's Digest version," Augusta chuckled.

"How do your singers like the opera?"

"Savitri and Death love it. Satyavan, not so much. He has some great music to sing, but he spends nearly half the opera dead."

Dennis slapped his knee and laughed again. "It sounds to me as if you've got a handle on this opera. It'll be interesting to see how your audiences respond."

"It will indeed. My job is to help them at least appreciate it."

"Anything else I can help you with? Though mainly, just understanding that world view—that all we experience in this life is an illusion, even death—seems to be what you mainly need to wrap your head around."

Augusta closed the score and leaned toward Dennis. "So different from the way the Western mind sees life. And what was that other concept—every soul has been here since the beginning? And experiences many lives as a result of reincarnation?"

"Transmigration is the preferred term. All of life is sacred, because that annoying bug you want to swat could be your great-grandmother."

She smiled, then grew serious. "That kind of world view, though—what would it be like to find yourself in a dreadful situation and to react with such calm? 'This is not real. I'm not really experiencing this, it's *maya*.'"

"You can understand the appeal."

"Oh, yes, actually, I can. So Savitri has that knowledge. Holst even says that at the end. Death is defeated by one who knows all of life is an illusion. And as I understand it, only God—Brahman—is real. Is life. And that's the way my soprano needs to see her character and what she must show to the audience."

"Exactly. You've got your work cut out for you, but if anyone can pull this off, it's Augusta McKee."

"Thanks, Father Dennis." She stood. "I'm beginning to get some staging and set ideas now. It's an exciting project. Appreciating it isn't enough. I want to see if I can get the audience to love it."

Dennis walked her to the door. "That's a tall order unless you love it."

"I love parts of it. My cast will be outstanding, and the audience will love what they do."

"That's the hallmark of an Augusta McKee production. By the way, how's your detective these days?"

"Struggling with a tough assignment. Hoping to close a case before it becomes a cold case. The murder of a fellow officer, four years ago."

She smiled wistfully. "I doubt I could convince Mal to look at this as the Eastern mind would. That everything is *maya*."

***

That conversation with Dennis had been three weeks earlier, and her cast was now deeply involved in preparing this unusual work for an early November performance.

She parked her car on Oak Street and went directly to the Recital Hall for that evening's rehearsal of *Savitri*. In addition to Nando Diaz as Death, her cast included another grad student as Savitri, Ginny McGuffee, who had come to them from Converse College. She had the big, powerful soprano voice the role demanded. Arthur Hayward, the tenor playing the husband, held his bachelor's degree from Howard University. He was one of the few Black students at the Conservatory, another young singer with a real chance at a career in opera. Augusta was impressed with the performances of these promising young singers, and she had meant what she said to Dennis: the audiences would respond well to what they would do with this unusual offering.

Another one-act opera would complete the evening: Puccini's delightful comedy *Gianni Schicchi,* directed by John Edmanston. An opera also about death, but a totally different take—a family of scheming relatives of a wealthy man who has just died. With the large cast for the Puccini opera and a chorus of twelve women in the *Savitri* ensemble, many of the voice majors in the school were involved.

The rehearsal this particular night was shared by both productions. Augusta finished working with her cast early, so the students took advantage of a few happy minutes to socialize as the *Schicchi* cast drifted into Recital Hall. Augusta watched them, thinking for this moment in time they were in something of a bubble— young men and women of varied backgrounds, for these few moments strongly united by their common passion for their art. *Life as it should be.*

After her talk with Dennis, she'd spent part of a rehearsal discussing the basis for Holst's opera with her cast, the Hindu concept of life and death. Their discussion broadened when Nando commented, "Professor McKee, those words I sing in the opera. It's what I've always understood about death—everybody dies."

Laughter throughout the cast, and Nando grinned and took a bow.

"Yes, we believe we die once," Augusta responded, "and hopefully, go to a better place. The Hindus believe the soul inhabits different bodies through many lives, and returns to this world repeatedly to learn new lessons. At least that's how I understand it."

Arthur chimed in. "The way I understand Christianity, there are two forces at work in this world, good and evil. If we choose good, we're charged to love God and to love our neighbor. Then in the scriptures, especially in the Old Testament, we're given a bunch of rules. Why is that? Why can't we just follow the directive to love God and to love others?"

Lily Myles, one of the girls in the ensemble, replied, "Because people do stupid stuff all the time. Bad stuff. We just can't seem to help ourselves."

"Well, the Hindus think that bad stuff isn't real," Nando observed. "It's an illusion."

"It sure feels real if you're on the receiving end of that bad action," Lily retorted tartly, causing them all to laugh.

Augusta glanced around the room again, recalling that discussion. *One thing all the world's religions agree on, so far as I understand, is that all of us have a soul. All of us are a soul—this body we're wearing doesn't survive. But in some way, the essence of the soul goes on.*

My mother's soul. The soul of the man buried in my neighborhood. Don Martin's soul.

84

Life and death. Good and evil.

How differently Westerners and Easterners view them.

Chapter 7
Wesley Vandergriff

Wednesday, October 27
4:00 p.m.

"I cleaned it again, and looking through a loupe you can just make out some indentations which might be the bottom part of the letters Reichenbach mentioned. Gold doesn't degrade, but this is 14 karat and the alloy it was mixed with has tarnished and degraded somewhat."

Gary Ridgeway handed the pocket watch, carefully nestled in a square of fabric, to Malcolm and offered him the eye piece.

Mal stared at the loupe and then at Gary, who laughed. "Hang on. How about a regular old magnifying glass?"

Sure enough, faint but visible Malcolm saw what might have been the very bottom part of the initials "W. V." in an ornate script. "I'd like Peter Reichenbach to take another look at this."

"We photographed it through a macro lens so you can take the picture to him rather than bringing him back here, if you'd like."

"That would be great. I need to spend some time interviewing him and having this will be a big help." The eight by ten photograph showed the markings on the watch even more clearly.

The next morning, Jim contacted Peter Reichenbach. Without telling him about the initials, he asked if they could meet with him again to discuss the case. Peter suggested they come to his home that afternoon around four, after he'd completed his day of teaching at the College of Mt. St. Joseph.

Indian Hill was an upscale area with large, almost baronial homes on spacious lots. The Reichenbach manse was a picturesque Victorian on manicured grounds. Peter responded to the bell and invited them into the library, where they met his wife. "Mary Ellen, these are the detectives I told you about—Malcolm Mitchell and Jim Edmonds."

Mal glanced around the room, noting several stacks of books on the floor and some empty shelves. *He must be reorganizing them.* A fire glowed and crackled in a large Rookwood fireplace with embossed tiles. A mahogany rolltop desk, more books piled high; a state-of-the-art stereo and next to it shelves crammed with albums of music. A comfortable sofa and several overstuffed chairs. The room definitely reflected its owner.

Mary Ellen Reichenbach, even in flat heels as tall as her husband, smiled warmly and extended a slender hand. "Welcome, gentlemen."

Brown hair, pretty brown eyes, probably five-ten. Attractive lady, Mal thought.

"May I offer you coffee and snacks?" She gestured toward a table which held a carafe, cups, sugar, cream, small plates, and an assortment of cheeses, crackers, and baguettes.

Peter remarked, "I wanted to offer you beer or wine, but Mary Ellen reminded me you're here officially since you're working. Maybe another time?"

"Nice meeting both of you. I'll leave you to talk." Mary Ellen turned to go.

"You're welcome to stay, Mrs. Reichenbach," Mal said. "You may remember something your husband told you at one time."

Jim filled a plate as he added, "This is really nice of you."

Once they were all comfortably seated, Mal removed the photo from the folder he had brought with him.

"Let's start with this. The coroner did a little more work on the pocket watch, and discovered there *are* initials. They're hard to discern after years being buried, but could this be the watch you remember seeing as a child?"

Peter took the photo and studied at it. "I don't know…it might be the watch I remembered. I thought the letters were…well, easier to see." He looked up at Mal. "They are difficult to make out, aren't they? But still…yes, I suppose this might be Uncle Wes's pocket watch. I called them 'fancy letters.'"

Baffled, he stared at both detectives. "But this can't be his watch. Wesley Vandergriff can't possibly be the bones you found. He's buried in Spring Grove Cemetery."

"He died in 1918?" Mal spread brie on a baguette.

"Not even a month after my mother. Wes had no family. He died of influenza in General Hospital, while my father was there. My dad took care of all the arrangements. It was such a dark time for him. He never liked to talk about it afterward."

"So sorry for your loss, Peter. I can't even imagine," Jim said.

"My mother is buried there as well. I didn't attend either funeral." Peter sipped his coffee. "Maybe I told you that my grandparents took me out of Cincinnati when my father told them things were going to get very bad. As I told Augusta, they wanted to take my mother as well, but she wouldn't leave my dad."

"Where did you go? No place was safe, from what I understand," Mal asked.

"I'm really not sure. I think Kentucky. We were in a rural area but fairly close to a city…maybe it was Lexington. I remember going into town a time or two. My aunt, my mother's sister, had a home there." Peter leaned forward. "My father came down right around Christmas, and then I went home with him. He really made an effort. He'd put up a tree and had toys for me. We talked about my mother not being there, and then he didn't say much more about it."

"What did he say about Wesley Vandergriff?" Jim asked.

"Just that the influenza was a terrible disease and a lot of people died. He was sorry he had to tell me Wesley was one of them. He took me to the grave when the stone he bought was set in place. I don't remember Dad ever talking about him after that."

"People deal with grief in different ways," Mary Ellen commented. "My father-in-law once told me he considered himself a stoic. He said he had to be."

"What do you remember about Wesley?" Mal asked Peter.

"He was so different from my dad. Dad was quiet. Serious. Wesley was one of the most exuberant people I've ever known. You know, he was on his way to becoming a world- famous organist—at least that's what I've been told—but he also was an incredible pianist. When he came to our house, he would always play. He loved exciting music. My favorite was something by Rachmaninoff. It was really the accompaniment for a song named 'Floods of Spring,' but he had turned it into a piano piece." Peter warmed to the subject. "My mom took me to a church once when he was practicing the organ. I'd never heard anything like it. He was working on something, transcribing a piece written for orchestra so he could play it on the organ."

"Augusta tells me you play the piano, as does your son," Malcolm commented.

"I'd have majored in music in college if my dad had agreed to it. He allowed me to take private lessons on piano through high school. I'm strictly an amateur, but my son is pursuing music as a career."

"What else do you remember about Vandergriff?" Mal poured himself another half cup of coffee.

"He was a giant. Well, he seemed to be, to a little boy, anyway. Extremely tall. One reason he played so well was because he had such long fingers. I'm not sure how tall he was. I'd bet at least six-four." He chuckled. "I said tall, but when I was a kid, I always told people my Uncle Wes was *long*. The longest person I'd ever seen."

Mal glanced at his watch. "Thanks so much for talking to us, Peter. And thank you for the refreshments, Mrs. Reichenbach."

"Mary Ellen, please, Detective. And give Augusta my best, will you?"

Once in the car, Jim said, "We should find the death certificate in the coroner's records, right? And the burial record at Spring Grove."

"Yes, we should. And if they check out, that will eliminate Wesley Vandergriff as our skeleton."

He drove quietly for a few minutes. "But it presents us with another mystery. If the watch is Vandergriff's, how did it end up buried in the Worthington's backyard?"

***

After Augusta finished her final voice lesson that afternoon, she sought out the two organ teachers on the Conservatory faculty to ask what they could tell her about Wesley Vandergriff. He hadn't been on the faculty at the Conservatory, and the school's library revealed little information.

I'll see what I can find in the Hamilton County library, she thought. *And I guess I can contact that annoying reporter, Arnold Richter, at The Cincinnati Morning Call. He may prove helpful for a change.*

Mal's car was already there when she arrived home, and since the house was empty it was apparent he had taken Fritz for a walk. She was staring into the refrigerator when she heard her boys come in through the back door, Fritz making a bee-line for her.

"Stay down!" She admonished automatically, and he sat, his tail thumping on the floor as he gazed at her expectantly. "Good boy." She patted his head.

"Not as good as he would like you to believe," Mal laughed. "When I got home there was a trail of unrolled toilet paper all the way up the stairs to the master bathroom. Fritz said he's real sorry but it seemed like a good idea at the time."

Augusta couldn't help but laugh, too. "Not the worst thing he's done…but really, Fritz, that was a bad boy." She tried to look stern, and Fritz briefly hung his head.

"So, are you hungry?" she asked Mal.

"Your friend Mary Ellen Reichenbach gave us snacks, and I demolished them pretty thoroughly," Mal chuckled. "How about something light? Soup and sandwiches works for me."

"Excellent idea. Tomato soup and grilled cheese?"

Mal had moved into the pantry with Fritz at his heels. Feeding Fritz meant filling his dish with dog food which disappeared almost as quickly as it was poured, and he always looked disappointed when the dish wasn't refilled.

The dog trotted back into the kitchen, again gazing expectantly at Augusta as she began to prepare the sandwiches. "No. You don't get any." Once in a while she would sneak him a piece of cheese, but if Mal caught her he would reprimand both her and the puppy.

"Don't hand feed him, Augusta. Bad idea. He'll just keep begging for more, and before you know it, we've got an overweight dog."

"Go lie down, Fritz." Tail between his legs, his eyes filled with sorrow, he slowly obeyed.

They completed their meal preparation in companionable silence and carried plates and bowls into the alcove, Augusta's favorite room in her house. It had been an addition at some point in the Tudor's history. The outside wall consisted almost entirely of a large bow window which overlooked Augusta's garden. A rustic dark oak table which comfortably seated four was the only furniture other than a phone stand against one inside wall. Glass French doors opened into the dining room. Watercolors of scenes of Cincinnati by a local artist, Robert Fabe, hung next to the French doors. The large kitchen behind the alcove had been part of the addition and a great selling point for Augusta when she bought the house some years earlier.

"I talked to both of the organ teachers." Augusta smiled slightly as she watched Fritz creep into the room and lie down against a wall, chin on his paws. She knew he would watch every bite they took.

"Of course, neither of them knew Vandergriff personally, but his reputation is kind of legendary here in Cincinnati. It's thought if he had lived, he might have been an even greater organist than E. Power Biggs."

"Okay, educate me. I don't know a thing about organists."

"Biggs is a British-born organist who has spent most of his life in the U.S. He's considered the best in the world, and has been performing and recording for decades."

"How old is he?"

"I think he's close to sixty. Of course, one of the reasons for his fame is the growth of the recording industry. But he's considered the greatest proponent of the pipe organ in the twentieth century."

"And your guys say Vandergriff was maybe even better?"

"Wesley Vandergriff was only thirty-two when he died. Yes, if he had survived, he'd have been performing worldwide over the next decades, and no doubt recording. Nathan Fischer told me Vandergriff had made a couple of old Gramophone recordings that very year—1918. He owns remastered copies and offered to play them for me."

"He'd let you borrow them?"

"No way. He'd let me come to his place and listen to them."

Mal grinned and shook his head. "There's an interesting approach. 'I don't have any etchings, so come up and hear my recordings, little girl.'"

Augusta almost spit out her mouthful of soup. "Hardly. Anyhow, Nathan's gay."

"Well, in that case, you're permitted to go."

Augusta punched Malcolm lightly on the shoulder. "I don't need permission, Detective."

"Sorry. Lost my head." He dipped a grilled cheese wedge into his soup. "Please continue."

"Nathan remembers hearing his teacher talk about Wesley. He was physically an imposing figure. Extremely tall, maybe six-feet-five. Slender, with unusually long fingers."

"Yes, Peter Reichenbach made that same comment. Only he said as a kid, he always thought of Wesley as long."

"The anecdotal history of the man includes that he was larger than life in other ways. One of those people everyone looked at when he walked into a room. Not pretentious, just somehow larger than life. Full of enthusiasm. Effusive might be a good word. Generous and witty. People liked him. Everyone loved him."

"He sounds like a genuinely fascinating character. Nobody's ever written a book about him?"

"Sadly, apparently not." A thought struck her. "You know, I may suggest that to Mary Ellen Reichenbach. She's a writer."

"Tell me more. I promise I'll quit interrupting."

"Physical description: good-looking man. Walked with a slight limp which was worse when the weather was bad. Nathan assumed he'd probably broken a bone at some point but didn't know that for a fact. He dressed rather flamboyantly."

She twisted in her chair to gaze at Malcolm directly. "He sounds like a charmer and apparently he didn't lack for female interest. Different companions, but no serious romance. I asked Nathan if it had been rumored he was gay, and he said definitely not. He loved women. But he was single when he died."

Malcolm wiped his mouth with his napkin. "All very fascinating, but I'm afraid for naught. He can't be our Mr. X, because Peter tells me Vandergriff was buried in Spring Grove Cemetery. Jim is checking that out tomorrow."

"Well, that's kind of a relief. I didn't like thinking Thomas Reichenbach had killed his best friend and buried him in his backyard. What could his motive have been, if that had been the case? I mean, especially a medical doctor. Sworn to do no harm."

"There is one little troublesome detail."

"Oh? What?"

"The pocket watch. It very well could have belonged to Wesley Vandergriff."

Chapter 8
Evil, Good, and Strange Music

Friday, October 29
9:00 a.m.

As Malcolm expected, records from the coroner's office and Spring Grove Cemetery confirmed that Wesley Vandergriff had died of influenza at General Hospital the third week of October in 1918. He was buried less than a week later. The death certificate was signed by Dr. Thomas Reichenbach, who paid for the cemetery plot, the coffin, and services of the funeral director.

They had a second possible suspect to investigate, and Jim's search of tax records at the Hamilton County Courthouse showed no current information for work by the contractor who had laid the patio in 1918, Bright and Sons Masonry.

"These independent contractors come and go," Jim commented when he returned to the office. "It's not surprising there's no 'Bright and Sons' still providing services all these decades later."

"Let's take a look at the Yellow Pages." Each of them opened a 1965 phone book.

Jim quickly ran a finger down the first page of "Stone Masons and Stone Work" listings. "Nope, no Bright and Sons. Now what?"

Mal frowned as he lifted the book and flipped the pages in that section. "Look at this list. There are pages and pages of them."

Jim snapped his fingers. "Hold on a second. Looky here what I just found. 'Davis and Bright, Stonemasons.' Well, well, well. Could be one of those sons." He grabbed his coat and almost ran from the office.

Heartened by even a hint of success, Mal made a quick call to Buck Grimes at the coroner's office and learned Gary was still continuing his painstaking examination of the bones. Malcolm was beginning to wonder if they would ever learn who the victim had been.

He thought it highly doubtful that Mr. Bright or one of his sons would have been stupid enough to kill someone and bury his body while on a job. It made more sense they would have been grateful for the job and done the work as quickly and efficiently as possible, especially given the circumstances of death and disease lurking everywhere.

On the other hand, anything is possible. I really like Peter Reichenbach. It would be nice to tell him his father wasn't responsible.

Frustrated, he pulled out the Don Martin file again. *What I'd like to do is talk to Jesse Walls. And to Anna Walls, Walt's wife.* He could find no record of any interviews of the elusive Mrs. Walls. Walt himself had been interviewed several times. Malcolm read on.

Detective Jerry Schrimph, Personal Crimes Squad investigator, was told by an informant that Walter Walls had bragged while in jail about killing Officer Don Martin. By then, the 29-year-old Walls was in the Ohio State Penitentiary for the third time. During 1958, he was sent there for altering car titles. He was paroled in 1959 and sent back again during January 1960 as a parole violator. On February 23, 1961 he was paroled again – two weeks before killing Patrolman Martin. Three months after the killing, he was caught carrying a firearm and sent back to prison.

There was more, but Malcolm had been through the file so many times he felt he had it almost memorized. It was entirely possible someone in Walls' family knew the truth but they were all in fear for their lives, so wouldn't tell what they knew.

He had a vivid recall of standing next to Don Martin's casket and silently vowing to bring his killer to justice. Though not a regular churchgoer, Malcolm considered himself a Christian, and he believed in redemption. But redemption required remorse and a desire to repent. So far as he could tell, Walls had neither of those. Malcolm also believed in an ongoing battle between good and evil, and he saw Walter Walls as one who had chosen evil. He could see not one redeeming quality about the man.

More frustration: at the moment, Mal had no idea how to locate Anna Walls. Talking to Jesse he knew was pointless. Walter's brother refused to answer any questions about him. Malcolm doubted talking to Anna would be any better, but he'd like a shot at it.

He picked up the phone to call Jesse's onetime parole officer, feeling it was probably an exercise in futility. *But I have to try. I have to close this case.*

***

Despite the cold drizzle outside, Augusta pulled on boots, bundled up well and picked up Fritz's leash. He was by her side in a flash, tail wagging. Fridays were a light day for her, and both her morning students had canceled their lessons because of illness.

"You don't mind a little damp, do you, Fritzy?"

She headed up the hill toward the Reichenbach/Worthington house, walking briskly. *I wonder if we possibly missed something. Anything. Probably not.*

She slowed as soon as she was almost in front of the house, Fritz happily sniffing everything he could reach.

A large Victorian with a touch of Italian or Greek Renaissance revival, the house undoubtedly the most imposing in the neighborhood. Her own graceful Tudor seemed modest by comparison. Augusta doubted there had been any structural changes over the past nearly fifty years, though she knew the kitchen had been modernized and the entire house rewired and replumbed. The exterior was faced with two shades of sandstone. A wide staircase led to an ornate entrance, double doors with elaborate stained glass in the top half, an archway above them. Intricate stonework around each window, and every room in the house had at least one, with several bay windows on the first floor.

The wide drive wound to the left side of the house and a double garage, which was a more recent construction but matched the house perfectly. Between the house and the garage was a gate which led to the patio in the backyard.

That must have been open last week when Fritz ran up here to dig. Just happenstance, she was sure. Peg or Charlie had been out on the patio and didn't completely close the gate when going back inside. Augusta imagined herself back in time, a dark night in October 1918. Whoever the victim was…possibly Wesley Vandergriff…was at the house for some reason.

Thomas had recently buried his wife. *An old friend stopping by to offer comfort?* And the next morning, the soil appearing undisturbed, the stonemasons had returned to complete their work. The perfect crime…for a long time.

"Come, Fritz." Augusta pulled briefly on the leash and Fritz trotted beside her obediently as they returned home. As they passed the house below the Worthingtons', she heard music coming from within. A recording of the overture to Bizet's opera *Carmen*. Happy memories of performing the role of Frasquita with the Cincinnati Summer Opera flooded back.

Not long after her first encounter with Malcolm two years earlier, he revealed to her that he saw her perform in *Carmen* the summer after he graduated from high school. He later admitted he'd been quite smitten with her. It was their private joke that whenever Augusta overstepped, it was actually the saucy gypsy Frasquita who made her do it.

His schoolboy crush on an older woman. She smiled at the thought, though the seven-year gap in their ages had concerned her at first. Mal had a failed first marriage and two sons. When Augusta met Carla—who had re-married quickly—it became apparent why the marriage hadn't worked. Both of Malcolm's sons, Ryan, now an attorney, and Danny, a member of the CPD, made it clear they saw Augusta as a second mother and the woman who had brought their dad the happiness they believed he so deserved. *I am truly blessed,* she thought.

A tug on his leash meant Fritz sensed Mal was home even before Augusta noticed his car in the driveway. Both of them ran the remainder of the way.

Once back in the kitchen, Augusta wrapped her arms around her husband, the love of her life, and buried her face against his shoulder.

"Wow. I just came home for lunch." He leaned back and grinned at her. "Maybe dessert as well?"

Mal helped her off with her coat and removed Fritz's leash, and he ran circles around both of them.

"I was just thinking about you." Augusta embraced her husband more tightly. "And then here you are."

"I had to get away from the office for a while." He leaned down to calm the puppy. "Looks like coming home was a great idea."

Augusta kissed him. "Dessert first. Lunch after," she murmured against his neck.

***

Jim was unwrapping a burger and fries at his desk when Malcolm returned to the office, and he looked closely at his partner. "Lunch at home, Detective Mitchell?" he smirked.

"Yes. And that's all that will be said about that," Mal grinned as he sat at his desk. "So, how was your interview?"

"We can rule out the mason as a suspect, but the interview was still productive. Herbert Bright was a seventeen-year-old kid in 1918. He was expected to answer the call of his country as soon as he turned eighteen, and was scared of both going overseas to fight in the trenches and of catching the Spanish flu. Those were pretty much foremost in his mind, but he did recall helping his dad install the Reichenbach patio." Jim took a hearty bite of burger.

"That must have been a scary time to be a boy of seventeen. I think the draft age was dropped to eighteen that September. How many millions of those kids went overseas, I wonder?"

"I remember that from somewhere. Nearly five million, but there were some women who were included in that number."

"What a waste. Trench warfare. Just killing people off, nobody could have ever won." Mal shook his head. "Anyway, you were saying?"

"Herbert remembers the job because his mother was a nurse at the hospital, so Dr. Reichenbach was a familiar figure to them. It was kind of unusual because they had started work, and then Dr. Reichenbach's wife died, so they were waiting to hear from him when he wanted them to come back. One morning he called before dawn and was in a hurry for them to finish up. He said his dad didn't ask questions because Reichenbach offered them a handsome amount to finish the patio that morning. So, they went to the house a couple of hours later and completed the installation."

"That's kind of too bad. It confirms Reichenbach as possibly a killer who wanted to cover up his crime as quickly as possible."

"Yeah. Herbert said they got to the house as soon as they could, and Reichenbach hung around until the stones—the gravel—and the sand had been poured and they were leveling it to lay the flagstones." Jim wadded up his food wrappers and pitched them into the trash can.

"So, Reichenbach left before they finished, then. He knew the body was concealed. And he had to get to the hospital, I would think."

"Hang on. There's more. Herbert remembered the stones they used. Almost three inches thick, bluish-gray limestone from Indiana, irregular shapes that he called 'natural flagging.' He said that's what they were laying in those days. Well, I called the mason the Worthingtons hired to lay the new patio on the off-chance he could tell me what they did with the stones they removed. They'd kept them to see if they could trim and re-use them. So, ol' Herb and I made a trip to see them, and he confirmed those were the exact stones."

"No kidding. Great work, partner. That removes any doubt."

"One final thing, Dr. Reichenbach gave Herb's dad payment in full before he left. In cash. But I guess back then that might not have been unusual."

Mal sighed. "I guess I need to share this with Peter. It wasn't what I had hoped to tell him."

"Yeah, I know. I like the guy, too."

Mal took a chance on catching Peter Reichenbach at home. Mary Ellen answered the door and greeted him cordially. "Peter's in the library. Is this an official visit or can I offer you a beer?"

"Maybe a pop? Ginger ale, if you have it. It's officially unofficial. I just have something I want to share with him."

She laughed. "Please go on in. You know your way."

Mal found Peter relaxing, listening to an instrumental piece of music that sounded dance-like and slightly spooky at the same time. Peter stood when Mal came in.

"You know, I was just thinking about you." The men shook hands. "This is a piece of music Wesley loved—Saint-Saens *Danse Macabre*. Highly appropriate for Halloween."

Mary Ellen appeared with Mal's ginger ale and a glass of white wine for herself.

"Since this is a quasi-social call, may I join you?"

"I'd be disappointed if you didn't." Mal replied.

Peter returned to his seat, waving a hand in time with the music. "Captivating, isn't it? It represents Death calling forth the dead on Halloween. That's Death playing the violin. And the xylophones represent rattling bones. Maybe skeletons dancing for him."

Malcolm lifted an eyebrow, somewhat taken aback.

Peter laughed, "You probably think it's weird that I'm listening to this, under the circumstances. But I love this piece. The composer received a lot of flak when he wrote it back in the eighteen-seventies. The critics claimed it caused people anxiety to listen to it. Now it's considered one of his best-known works."

He smiled wistfully. "The first time I heard it was when Wesley adapted it for organ, but I don't think he ever got to perform it."

"It's…intriguing," Mal said cautiously.

"What's intriguing are my family's bones," Peter grinned. "Of course, I mean the ones your dog found."

"They certainly are. That's why I'm here." He leaned forward. "We found one of the men who built the patio back in 1918, Herbert Bright. He was a kid working for his father then, and he's still working as a mason."

"Let me guess: there was nothing suspicious about his story."

Malcolm nodded. After a long moment Peter continued, "I mean, my dad actually contracted with them to build the patio…and they had no idea they were covering up a body."

"That does seem to be what happened. But we don't know the circumstances, Peter. Those were turbulent times. There could be any number of reasons why the body was concealed."

The music ended, and Peter slowly rose and turned off the stereo. "It's hard to imagine what they might have been, Mal." He sighed and sat down again, Mary Ellen moving to his side and placing a sympathetic hand on his shoulder.

"I have to accept that for some reason, my father most likely dug a grave one night in October 1918, buried a body, and made sure it was concealed…he hoped forever. And we probably will never know whose body it was and why he did it, will we?"

"Most likely we won't." Malcolm finished his drink and rose to leave. "But Gary is still working on the bones. He may yet come up with something which will make it possible for us to figure this out."

"Look, Mal." Peter rose and pointed a finger at Malcolm. "My dad was a great father to me, and a great grandfather to my kids. He did a lot of good in his profession, he saved a lot of lives. And after he retired, he rendered service to our community—and to our country—however he could."

Peter paused and swallowed hard. "You know, a lot of people have a dark secret in their past. That doesn't mean they were evil. What I'm holding on to is all the good Dr. Thomas Reichenbach did in his life."

Chapter 9
Illusion and Reality

Saturday, October 30

Malcolm had a rare day off on Saturday, but Augusta had a meeting that morning with her technical director for the opera performances which were scheduled for the following weekend. She also had a rehearsal on Sunday from two until seven, so wouldn't be able to spend much time at home.

On a crisp, sunny, late fall day, they enjoyed a large, leisurely breakfast, bookended by Mal walking Fritz before and after. Sipping a second cup of coffee, Augusta mused, "It seems to me Peter Reichenbach might be taking this a little too well. From what you said, he's accepted that his father did this…buried a body and covered it over with a patio."

"I agree with you. It's not real to him yet. I understand him not wanting to dishonor his father's memory, but this has all the attributes of a possible

111

homicide. And Jim and I have to follow wherever it leads."

"Do you have any idea when Gary will finish his examination?"

"He said he hoped to complete his report by Monday. Not that we may learn anything more than we already know."

Augusta took cups into the kitchen and rinsed them. "If I get going, I might be home for lunch. I only need to check Larry's lighting cues. He certainly doesn't need me standing around while he hangs and focuses the lights."

Mal kissed her and helped her on with her coat, Fritz trotting up to her and looking at her expectantly, tail wagging.

"I guess when I put a coat on, he expects a walk." She ruffled the dog's head. "Have a good time at school, Fritz." She glanced at Malcolm. "Talk to his teacher about that taste he's developed for feathers, will you?"

"He'll probably suggest we forego feather-stuffed pillows," Mal laughed. "What would you like to do about lunch?"

"After all the food we just ate? Maybe an early supper. Why don't we go out? We could see if Milly and Garrett would like to join us. Maybe at Lenhardt's?"

"Sounds good. I'll give them a call."

***

Augusta had given a great deal of thought as to how to stage the Holst opera. She read that the composer requested it be presented in an outdoor setting, and specifically, a woodland setting. It seemed as if he realized it was highly unusual operatic fare, especially for the Victorian era in which it was written.

It also intrigued her that he had chosen to write the text in English as it had been spoken centuries earlier, the language of the King James Bible and the Anglican Book of Common Prayer. All of this influenced her to stage it as not realistic, but impressionistic. A few weeks earlier she had talked to Larry Rodgers, the professional set designer and tech she often worked with, about her staging ideas.

"Let me guess." He gave her a lopsided grin. "You don't have any money."

"Well…not much," she laughed. "You know me too well. I've explained the plot, and why I don't think realism would work at all. Here's my vision: a painted scrim. Maybe woods or a grove of trees, something like that. If it's not too realistic, that would be wonderful. And I think that's all we need on stage."

Warming to the subject, Augusta continued to describe her staging ideas to a talented stage technician who could help her bring them to life. "We backlight Fernando—Death—behind the scrim so we see this large, looming shadow. Savitri enters from one side and she's in front of the scrim. The female ensemble is behind it, and we bring light up on them when they sing. Satyavan enters from the rear of the auditorium."

Larry nodded, busily making notes.

"When Satyavan falls, dead, and Death sings again, we use the backlight. But the backlight fades as he comes downstage and through the scrim, and he's not this frightening figure we thought he was, but a man. Well, a Hindu god appearing as a man. Oh, the scrim needs to be divided, I guess I didn't mention that."

"No, you didn't."

"I think dimmed stage lights and follow spots on Savitri and Death during this section. Then when Death leaves, after Savitri has defeated him, he exits through the rear of the auditorium. Satyavan is revived, the ensemble comes in front of the scrim and we have full light on stage. I'm still deciding where to have Death sing his final lines."

"Come with me." Larry pulled her up and led her into his workshop, where several backdrops were hanging. He moved some forward to reveal a scrim painted as a grove of tall, slender trees.

Augusta gasped. "Oh, it looks like a Monet painting. Just what I dreamed of."

"Well, it was inspired by Monet, his painting 'Poplars at Giverny.' We did it for a production of *A Midsummer Night's Dream* about four years ago in Dayton. Is this kind of what you had in mind?"

"It's exactly what I had in mind. Will it fit our stage?"

"We may have to double it under on the sides, but that's not a big deal. The tormentors will cover it." He extended a hand and grinned at her. "Do I get an ad in the program?"

"Full page." Augusta hugged him.

"This'll be fun to light. What about costumes?"

"I'm going to keep them simple. Drapes in soft greens for the ensemble. Something brighter for Savitri and Satyavan—maybe rose and purple. And I think I want Death in white, not black. Loose-fitting pants and a knee-length jacket, maybe."

"I like your vision, Augusta."

"Oh, good. I hoped you would. Well, I'm off. I need to visit Jerry Westover at the Parkside Playhouse to see if he'll let me raid his wardrobe department."

Larry laughed. "Does the Conservatory realize how much money you save them on your productions?"

"Probably not. I do what I do because I love it. And I can't always get by on as much of a shoestring as for this one. Sometimes I do need you to build something for us."

"I've wondered how you manage that."

"I visit wealthy people and promise them a happy afterlife if they'll sponsor the set. And an effusive thank you in the program."

"You mean like the one you're giving me?" he laughed.

"No, you get a full-page, four-color ad. Let's hope it will bring you many paying customers."

Recalling how much pleasure it had given her to envision her production, Augusta thought, *I know how blessed I am to be able to let my imagination roam free, and hopefully, to give my singers an opportunity to provide moments of beauty and inspiration to the audience. The music in our lives helps us all deal with the real world.*

***

When she arrived at the Conservatory's Recital Hall, Larry already had the scrim hung and trimmed. "You can see we had to double it at each side, but the tormentors hide it."

"Just as you said they would." She walked the length of the scrim, touching it occasionally. "It looks gorgeous."

"It'll look better once I get the right lights on it. We have to move these around a bit." He gestured expansively at the lighting instruments hanging above the stage.

"As you always do," she smiled. "Shall we review the lighting plot?"

They sat together for nearly an hour until Larry was satisfied he understood exactly what she wanted to see at each point in the opera. "We can make any adjustments during the tech run-through tomorrow. I'm going to try to make this plot work in conjunction with John Edmanston's opera. I don't foresee any major problems. His requests are traditional. Mainly, we'll ditch the backlight and have more fixtures we'll use upstage. I have extra lighting instruments we can hang if we think we'll need more."

Augusta glanced at her watch. *Just a little after two.* On a whim, she headed for the John Roebling Suspension Bridge and Northern Kentucky. Nathan Fischer had suggested she talk to a legendary organist from an earlier era, who had been Wesley Vandergriff's teacher for a time.

Titus Powlett was now in his early nineties, residing in a nursing home on the outskirts of the charming town of Florence. Augusta considered herself fortunate to have performed at Christ Episcopal Church under his direction several times not long after she joined the Conservatory faculty. A consummate musician, Titus had shared his extensive knowledge in three books on organ technique and literature, and also had to his credit a unique recording: organ pieces played on the instruments located in several important Cincinnati and Covington churches.

The nursing home was spacious and airy, and the receptionist smiled pleasantly as Augusta approached the desk. "Good afternoon. How nice to see you. Who are you here to see?" Augusta was a little surprised that she was not in any kind of uniform, though perhaps she wasn't a medical person. *Of course, I don't spend much time in nursing homes.*

"I don't have an appointment. I was hoping for a visit with Mr. Powlett. Mr. Titus Powlett."

"You're in luck. He's actually in the visitor's lounge with some of the other residents. They often get together to play cards. May I let him know you're here?"

"Please. Augusta McKee." *I hope he remembers me. I should have asked Nathan if Titus' memory is still good.*

She needn't have been concerned, because moving fairly briskly for a man on a walker, Titus returned with the receptionist. He beamed at her. "Augusta, what a wonderful surprise! Imagine you coming all this way to see me!"

Despite the thinning white hair and thick glasses, he looked much the same as she remembered him.

"I'm so happy you have some time, Titus. I should have been to visit sooner." *And do I ever feel guilty that I've never been here before.*

Almost as if he'd read her mind, Titus said quickly, "Nonsense. Why would you? We didn't have a close connection, though I always enjoyed the opportunity to work with you back when I was still at Christ Church. And I appreciated your gift when I retired."

He led her to a quiet corner in the busy lounge, where families and friends were gathered in groups with loved ones. A spinet piano stood against a wall in one corner, giving Augusta a sudden thought.

"That piano—a Baldwin Acrosonic, isn't it?"

"It is indeed. And it's kept in tune. I fiddle around with stuff sometimes, though I can't play as I used to. Would it surprise you to learn I've even written a few pieces?"

"That's..." She stopped, not sure what an appropriate expression would be.

"...surprising?" He chuckled. "It sure is, considering most people at my age do well to remember their names."

They laughed together. "Old age isn't a lot of fun, Augusta, but I'm one of the lucky ones. I remember everything. I had a great life, and I'm trying to enjoy it for as long as I can. Everybody thought Queen Victoria was old when she died, and I've got her beat by ten years."

"I know you toured Europe and performed at Westminster Abbey. Did you meet her?" *What a life this man has enjoyed.*

"I did. I was presented at court. Quite a thrill."

"And did you meet any of the great composers of that era? I'm in the process of directing a chamber opera by Gustav Holst."

He snorted. "The Conservatory is putting on *Savitri*? What on earth for?"

Augusta laughed heartily. "I actually am enjoying it. But it will never be a favorite, I have to admit."

"That was my second trip to England, and I saw the premiere. He wanted the silly thing performed out-of-doors but it was the dead of winter. I asked him whatever possessed him to write something based on a Sanskrit poem. He should have stuck with works inspired by English folk tunes. Though I have to admit, *The Planets* is pretty darned great."

"I've read that he was intrigued with Eastern mysticism and that he even studied Sanskrit."

"That whole British Raj thing. You know, I think a great many of the British had at least subconscious guilt about what they did to India." He leaned forward. "But I don't think you drove all this way to discuss Gustav Holst and British India with me."

"You're right. I came to ask what you remember about Wesley Vandergriff."

Titus' eyes brightened behind the thick glasses. "Best organ student I ever had. *Much* better than me. I felt privileged to teach the boy. And best of all, as the years passed, he also became a friend."

119

"I've been told he was exceptional."

"He was every bit of that. Tragic that he died so young. He'd have been the greatest organist of this century."

"I've heard that as well. What are your personal memories, though? I'm planning to suggest a biography of him to a friend." *And I will. Mary Ellen Reichenbach, get ready.*

"You know, there are some people who have this amazing ability to embrace all of life, no matter what it brings."

"I believe I'm speaking with such a person at this moment."

She was rewarded with a warm smile. "That's sweet. I try. But Wes didn't have to try. Everything about life thrilled him. He had this great ability to lift people up, whether by his playing or just being around him."

"I'm told he was quite tall."

"He was six feet five. Actually, he had a medical condition, and he learned about it when he broke his leg. It was a compound fracture and it took a long time to heal. In fact, it never healed completely."

"What was the condition?"

"It's called Marfan's Syndrome. His bones were unusually long. Those long fingers were one reason he played so well."

Augusta felt as if she had struck gold. "I've never heard of it."

"Most people don't know about it, but it's thought some famous historical figures had the same condition. Abraham Lincoln, for one. Niccoló Paganini. Those long fingers would also be a bonus to a violinist, and Paganini was legendary, as you know."

Titus suddenly yawned so hard his eyes watered. His head dropped for a brief moment before he jerked it upward. "Sorry, Augusta. I'm afraid my keeper is about to show up and take me away for a nap."

"Don't apologize, Titus. I think I overstayed my welcome. But I do want to ask you one quick question. I thought of this when I saw the piano. Do you think I might bring some of my students here to present a short recital for the residents? It would be a nice opportunity for my younger students especially."

Again, Titus' eyes shone. "Augusta, that would be absolutely wonderful."

"I promise I'll come back so we can discuss this more." She took his hand in hers, aware of the ravages of age in his gnarled fingers.

He squeezed her hand hard. "I hope you do."

She leaned forward and kissed his cheek.

"I never break a promise."

Chapter 10
What It Was Like

Augusta arrived home to find Garrett's car in the driveway. She went inside and was pleasurably surprised to be greeted by wonderful aromas.

"Change of plans," Milly informed her as they embraced. "I'm experimenting with Greek cuisine. Mal said he'd be a taste tester and thought you wouldn't mind."

"I'm a willing volunteer for your Greek food sensory panel."

"The men took Fritz for a walk. Garrett was intrigued to see the house where the extremely cold case murder mystery is unfolding."

"How much did Malcolm tell you?" Augusta asked.

"Very little, since he's been assigned to the case. Garrett has snooped around, though, and learned the coroner has bones in his lab and it's thought they might belong to Wesley Vandergriff. I asked him to tell Malcolm some people in the music community remember attending a memorial for Wesley at Spring Grove. The local organists collected money for a very nice monument which was placed on his grave."

"I plead the Fifth." Augusta went to the kitchen. "White or red? Which goes with Greek cuisine?"

"Both, technically, depending on the specific dish. I prefer white with this food, though."

"How many dishes do you have going?"

"Three. *Spanakopita*—spinach pie. *Moussaka*, which is eggplant with seasoned ground lamb and whipped potatoes, and is my favorite. And I have some grilled chicken and vegetable kebabs for an appetizer. Not exactly Greek, but close enough, and a little lighter."

"Pinot grigio sounds like a good pairing." Augusta poured a glass for each of them. "You're amazing. Please don't tell me you made that thin phyllo crust yourself for the spinach pie."

"I'm not that ambitious, or that good," Milly laughed. "Though Olga swears it's really not that hard to make. Of course, she learned at her grandmother's knee." Olga Tsapatoris was the proprietor of a new Greek restaurant in downtown Cincinnati, and it was no surprise to Augusta that Milly was on a first-name basis with her.

"What can I help you with? I just realized I'm starving. Mal and I had a late breakfast, but that was hours ago. I'd offer to set the table, but I see some nice person has already done that."

"The kebabs are ready. You can toss the salad and I'll get those onto the table. The dogwalkers should be back shortly." Milly opened the oven and even more amazing aromas were released.

"Of course, you remember Titus Powlett." Augusta placed the salad on the table. "I went over to Florence to visit him this afternoon after Larry and I were finished."

"How is he? He's been in that facility for six years now, I believe."

"Yes, he has. It's lovely, by the way, and I should have gone before now. I have such respect for him. He's sharp as a tack and still very witty." Augusta sipped her wine. "I'm planning to take some students over there to present a short recital. How would you feel about playing for us? There's a nice little Baldwin Acrosonic spinet in the visitor's lounge."

Milly arranged the kebabs across a platter. "I'd be happy to do that. What a nice thought."

Before Augusta could talk to Milly further about her visit with Titus, they were interrupted by the men returning with Fritz, who whined and pulled at his leash, eager to greet Augusta. She joined them in the back-entrance hall and fussed over her pup until he settled down.

Mal took Fritz into the pantry to feed him and Garrett followed Augusta to the kitchen. "I viewed the scene of the crime. Quite a house Dr. Reichenbach built for himself back in the day." Milly's beau cut an imposing figure, primarily because of his shock of white hair and air of confidence. Garrett more often than not won the difficult cases he accepted.

"The subsequent owners have certainly kept the house in good condition. It's kind of the neighborhood castle."

Garrett laughed. "I can see why Charlie and Peggy Worthington are very proud of it."

"How do you know them? Oh, let me guess. You've consulted with him on at least one case."

Garrett picked up a serving platter as they moved to the alcove dining table and seated themselves.

"More than one. He's a great witness. The prosecution knows they're in trouble when Dr. Charles Worthington takes the stand," Garrett chuckled.

The four of them dug into Milly's latest venture in the culinary arts and there was little talk for a time other than murmurs of "Oh. Oh. OH." "Oh, this is amazing." And an occasional "This is SO good."

Mal put on coffee as the other three cleared the table, put away leftovers, and took turns washing, drying, and stacking dishes. All four carried coffee into the living room and sank into a piece of furniture to relax.

"I'm convinced," Mal commented, leaning back in the sofa and extending his long legs as Augusta joined him and Fritz curled up at their feet. "Greek food is great."

"Well, don't just judge it by my first try, Malcolm," Milly said. "Visit Olga's for lunch or dinner, she needs customers. I have to admit to tailoring the recipes slightly to my taste."

"Why Greek, Milly?" Augusta inquired.

"It's just something I've never tried before. Always looking for a new cuisine to try out. I think I have Italian food down pretty well."

Murmurs of agreement. Milly was well-known for her Italian dinners and friends vied for reservations when she provided such a meal for a musical cause.

"Back to the Worthington house and the foul play in the backyard," Garrett said. "I know you can't talk specifics, Mal, but I understand the crime may have been committed as long ago as 1918." He shook his head. "Such a difficult year, with the war still going on and the epidemic raging. Death everywhere. I was only twelve, but I remember it as a frightening time."

"I was eight in 1918," Milly responded.

"I was eight as well," Augusta said. "I knew so little about the so-called 'Spanish flu,' even though my mother died of the disease that year. I did some reading at the library, newspaper articles from the period. In 1918, the entire world was in the grip of a terrible health crisis. In this country, Woodrow Wilson never even addressed the fact that people were dying by the thousands of a viral influenza. I found that surprising, but all he cared about was winning the war he had resisted being part of for years. Once he committed to the war, that was his entire focus. News was controlled. The important thing was keeping everybody's spirits up."

Milly brought coffee from the kitchen and refilled everyone's cup. "You know, it's odd. People survived that epidemic...well, I guess pandemic is the correct word...but I never heard much about it as a child," she said. "My family members who lived through it said very little. In fact, I've never given it much thought."

"Peter Reichenbach said pretty much the same thing, only it's now become part of his existence," Mal remarked. "His mother died in 1918 when he was a kid, same as Augusta's. And of course, his father was a physician caring for people for long, difficult weeks and months. But afterwards his father never spoke of it." He put down his coffee cup. "I don't recall my parents ever discussing it."

"Well, I do," Garrett said. "My mother was a nurse. She talked about it a lot. She was traumatized by what she experienced. She contracted the disease and survived it. I could tell you about what it did to people, what she saw specifically, but it's hardly suitable after-dinner conversation. Just let me say this. It was nothing like the 'flu' as we think of it. It was far, far worse. People could be fine in the morning and dead by midnight…or even earlier. Thousands of young men were shipped overseas when they were unwell to fight on the front lines, carrying the disease and infecting their shipmates. Some never even made it onto shore."

The room was still as Garrett continued, "In the U.S., it came in waves. It's thought it started somewhere in Kansas and soon traveled to an army training camp in that state. From there it went all through the country. That was in the early spring. Then in the summer, it seemed to die out. But it came back with a vengeance in the fall. Eventually so many people were infected and hospitalized civil authorities had to start closing down schools. Some churches closed their doors. Most large events were canceled. But in Philadelphia, a big rally was held, a women's parade to help the war effort. Thousands attended. Then thousands started dying. The hospitals were overwhelmed. The coroners couldn't keep up with the urgent requests to pick up bodies for burial. Like a scene from the dark ages—priests going through the streets with horse carts, collecting the dead.

"The virus continued to spread. People were told to stay home. Police and emergency personnel started wearing face coverings. Those became mandatory for everyone. Still people were infected, and near the end people didn't even want to look at those they passed on the street because that person might be infected and give the virus to them."

"Dear Lord. What would it be like to have to live that way?" Augusta glanced around at her friends. "To suspect the people you love of being able to unknowingly give you a disease that could kill you?"

Garrett finished his coffee. "My point is this— whatever Thomas Reichenbach may have done during that horrendous time in our history, he was dealing with a situation none of us can begin to comprehend. The man was a heroic figure, working tirelessly day and night in that hospital. Physicians are trained to save lives; it's difficult to believe he could have taken one. And if he did kill someone, there must have been some serious extenuating circumstances to explain such a terrible lapse in judgment."

He paused for a moment. "If he were alive today and charges were brought, I would defend him in a heartbeat, based on who he was and what he accomplished."

Garrett glanced at each of them, holding Mal's gaze for a long moment, as if he were expecting Mal to challenge what he had just said.

Mal didn't comment, and Garrett continued, "Hopefully, none of us will ever know what it was like during that time. We've had plagues all through history. The 1918 plague was bad, but it wasn't the worst. The Black Death holds that place, I believe."

They were quiet. Mal finally said, "You're saying it could happen again."

"I've been told it's not a matter of if, but when. I just hope the world is better prepared."

Chapter 11
A Case of Mistaken Identity

Monday, November 1
10:00 a.m.

Gary Ridgeway handed Mal a folder. "Here are my complete findings, but I know you'd like to hear a summary before you have to wade through all the details." He leaned against his desk and folded his arms over his chest.

"Thanks to some impressive police work, we know the remains were buried in late October, 1918, forty-seven years ago, and the shallow grave was covered over by sand, gravel, and limestone flagstones. It was undisturbed until earlier this month.

"Examination of the bones indicate the victim was a male of between twenty-five and thirty-five, six feet five inches in length. There were a few missing bones from the extremities, that is, hands and feet, but for the most part the skeleton was intact.

"The skull did not show any signs of trauma, but the roof of the mouth—the palate—was unusually high and arched, and consequently, there was some crowding of the teeth.

"The bones of the arms, legs, fingers, and toes were unusually long."

He stopped reciting his findings and commented, "In fact, they were so much so that I took a closer look at them. I found that the arm span was greater than the individual's height."

Mal raised a hand. "Arm span?"

"Yes. The measurement from the tips of the fingers of one hand to the tips of the fingers of the other hand. That measurement was six feet seven inches, therefore greater than six feet five. And along those same lines, I discovered a positive wrist sign. In other words, when this man was alive if he had encircled his wrist with the opposite hand, the thumb and little finger would overlap."

"And that told you what?"

"Because of the high soft palate, the crowded teeth, the long arm span, and the positive wrist sign, I believe I can say with certainty that our victim suffered from a condition known as Marfan Syndrome. It's very rare and is just beginning to be more thoroughly understood."

"What about the fracture of his left leg?"

"It doesn't appear to have healed correctly. I would say it was broken when he was maybe in his late teens or early twenties. It's possible the Marfan Syndrome was a contributing factor in the incomplete healing."

"We'll come back to that." *Titus Powlett told Gus that Vandergriff had this condition. But this can't be Vandergriff.* "Do you know how he died?"

"From a knife wound." Gary motioned Malcolm and Jim over to the examining table. "His throat was slit. You see the v-shaped nick on this bone, which is just below his chin. It took a very sharp knife to do this. A surgical knife, not a scalpel, exactly like the knife we found."

"So that kind of confirms Dr. Reichenbach as the killer," Jim said. "Sad."

"I'd say so, yes." Gary turned to them again. "Why he killed this man, and who he was, may forever remain a mystery."

"I'd agree with that, except for one thing. I learned over the weekend that Wesley Vandergriff suffered from Marfan's Syndrome."

"Marfan Syndrome," Gary corrected automatically. "Where did you learn that?"

"You know who Titus Powlett is, right?"

"Yes, of course. I heard him play many times. I know he's living down in Florence these days. He has to be over ninety."

"You may know this as well, he was Vandergriff's organ teacher. Augusta spent some time with him on Saturday, and that's one thing he told her."

Gary pushed his glasses up on his nose. "What else did he tell her?"

"That Vandergriff learned of his condition when he broke his leg. He was told that's why it took so long to heal, and never healed correctly."

"There's no way to confirm that," Jim commented. "Medical records are seldom kept much more than ten years after death."

The three men stared at each other. "Well, if this is Wesley Vandergriff, who's the imposter buried in that coffin in Spring Grove Cemetery?" Gary said.

"This *has* to be Vandergriff," Mal argued. "The pocket watch is the clincher. Why would Titus Powlett make up something about his former student having a rare bone disorder if it weren't true?"

"Only one way to find out," Jim said. "Exhume the body in Spring Grove."

Gary appeared glum. "Oh, great." It was common knowledge that was a part of his job Gary disliked intensely.

"The prosecutor's office can get a court order fairly quickly," Mal said. "With what we have, this should be a slam dunk. One good thing, we won't have to ask permission from the family. There's no one."

"Yeah, that's kind of sad," Jim commented. "Well, I'll get the ball rolling. I guess we're on hold until we're able to get a look inside that coffin."

"Let's not say anything to Peter as yet," Mal cautioned. "This is getting complicated."

"I don't know about that," Jim said. "Peter is the closest thing Wesley Vandergriff has to family. Maybe he should be consulted, as a courtesy if for no other reason."

"Hmm. What do you say, Gary?"

"I have to agree with Jim. You want to dot all your 'I's and cross all your 'T's, Mal. This is a highly unusual situation."

Mal sighed. "Okay, you're no doubt right. So, we'll consult Peter and receive his not-really-necessary permission to exhume the body. Hopefully, he'll agree right away."

***

They looked over Vandergriff's death certificate again before driving to the Reichenbach's that afternoon. Date, place of death, name of deceased, cause of death indicated as "complications from influenza." Since he died at General Hospital, it wasn't unusual that Dr. Reichenbach had signed the certificate, especially given the confusion of the times.

Jim had done some research and told Mal, "It seemed like nobody was in charge. Or everybody tried to take charge. There were no directives from the federal government, and for the most part, not even from state governments. Locally, there was a lot of back-and-forth between the city and county governments. It was a mess."

"Apparently. Who would have been prepared for a worldwide health crisis that infected millions of people that fall?"

Peter answered the door and ushered them into the living room. "I can see you have some news. I'm going to guess Coroner Ridgeway completed his examination."

"Peter, this won't be easy to hear," Mal said. He related the information about the unusual attributes of the skeleton, and reported on the comment from Vandergriff's former teacher. "Because of that, and the pocket watch which also points to Wesley Vandergriff, the coroner believes there is a possibility those are his remains."

"But there's something more that needs to be done to confirm it." Peter said.

"Yes. We have a death certificate for Vandergriff. And the person so identified was buried in Spring Grove Cemetery not long after his death," Jim said. "The coroner needs to exhume that body in order to confirm it is Wesley Vandergriff who is buried there."

Peter looked from one to the other. "Why are you telling me this? I'd think you'd have taken steps to exhume the body already."

Mal leaned forward. "The first step in exhumation is to request permission from the next of kin. While you're not a blood relative of Wesley Vandergriff, you're the closest thing to one. We feel you should be extended that courtesy."

"I see."

"Once we confirm that Vandergriff is buried in Spring Grove Cemetery, then we move forward on a John Doe murder. Since it took place so long ago during turbulent times, we may never learn who the victim was. Nor exactly what happened that led to the remains being buried where we found them."

"How did he die?"

Jim and Malcolm exchanged glances. "He did not die of natural causes," Jim said.

"So he was murdered."

Peter dropped into a chair, wiping his sweaty face with a shaking hand. "My father quite possibly murdered someone, and then concealed his crime."

"We don't know that yet," Jim said. "There certainly could be another explanation."

Peter was silent for a moment. "I'll have to think about this." He stood abruptly. "I need some time."

Both detectives got to their feet. "That's understandable," Jim said.

"If the body is exhumed, it's bound to become news. In any event, my father's name is going to be dragged through the mud. If Wesley isn't in that coffin, he falsified a death certificate. If Wesley *is* in the coffin, who was the man who was murdered? And why?"

"Yes, the need to exhume the coffin certainly complicates the situation," Mal said. "But this has to be done, Peter."

"Suppose I say no. Will you go ahead and exhume the body anyway?"

"Let's not get ahead of ourselves," Mal replied. "Take some time; it's not urgent. I'm sure you'll want to discuss this with Mary Ellen."

Peter walked briskly to the door to show them out. He stopped and stared hard at each of them. "Just think about this. What would you do if it were your father?"

Neither man could answer him.

Chapter 12
Fritz, Son of Caruso…
and Other Things

Wednesday, November 3

When Malcolm asked Augusta if they could provide foster care for Trevor Davidson's Golden Shepherd, Caruso, she had agreed with no little trepidation. Augusta had never had a pet. But Trevor had been severely wounded in the summer of 1964 while working a drug bust with Mal, and would need a few months to recover. He had no family locally to care for his dog. Caruso moved in.

Augusta grew to love the sweet, bright, endearing animal during his time with them, despite his penchant for chewing on her beloved stilettos. And Caruso had, in fact, saved her life by leading Malcolm to her location when she was kidnapped the following fall.

One thing she enjoyed most was Caruso's reaction to her singing. He would sit by the piano, waiting eagerly for her to hit a high note. And without fail, he'd join in with a mighty howl. Malcolm found it hysterically funny, and Augusta did as well. Bit by bit Caruso won her heart, and she'd been a little sad to see him leave, though Trevor dropped by occasionally with his dog and they always loved seeing both of them.

Fritz, who had been sired by Caruso, was Augusta's gift to Malcolm. Caruso was three years old when they cared for him, and training a puppy proved an entirely different experience. But with Malcolm's assistance and that of her combination housekeeper-dog sitter Henrietta Bluefield, it worked out better than she had anticipated. She made sure Fritz had an abundance of chew toys, though, and carefully put her stilettos away rather than kicking them off and leaving them on the floor, something she'd done much too often when Caruso was their foster dog.

Not long after Fritz joined the household, Augusta was curious to see how he would react to her playing and singing. She sat at the piano and began to play quietly. Fritz, fascinated by her feet on the pedals, growled and rushed at them. Augusta took her feet off the pedals and Fritz settled down. He sat next to the piano bench with his head cocked to one side, gazing at her quizzically.

She started to sing, softly at first, and his ears picked up. Completely expecting a Caruso-type howl from Fritz, Augusta sang a high note. Immediately the pup dropped his chin to the floor, whimpering, paws on each side of his head, as if to try to block out the noise.

Malcolm was watching and he and Augusta were convulsed with laughter. She scooped up the little puppy and hugged him, taking him into the pantry for a treat. She waited for a day, tried again, and received the same reaction. "Oh, dear. Sorry, puppy. You'll have to somehow get used to that horrible noise, because it's what I do."

Over the past four months he had stopped reacting quite so strongly, though at times he slunk out of the room when she sat down to practice. In recent days, though, he had stayed put, staring at her as if trying to figure out exactly why she wanted to make those sounds that hurt his ears.

Malcolm finished putting away the dinner dishes and wandered into the living room, Fritz at his heels. He relaxed onto the sofa, listening as Augusta played softly.

"Pretty. What is it?"

"It's a hymn by Gustav Holst, 'In the Bleak Midwinter.' A favorite of mine. One of the pieces Titus Powlett was talking about when he said Holst should have stuck with English folk music."

"Speaking of Holst, when do I have a ticket for the opera workshop performance?"

"Friday. Thank you for agreeing to come, by the way. You won't love *Savitri*, but I believe you'll enjoy the Puccini opera."

Malcolm laughed. "You may be selling me short. I might surprise you."

"Yes, and the sun rises in the west and sets in the east. And fairies materialize out of pixie dust on Fountain Square. Trust me on this one."

She moved to the sofa and snuggled against him as she caressed the back of his neck. "These two cases haven't been easy for you. From what you told me, even if Peter agrees to exhuming the coffin in Spring Grove, nothing can happen before Monday."

"That's true." He gazed into her eyes, the intense blue stare that turned her insides to mush and always had. "What are you leading up to?"

"Why do you think I'm leading up to something?"

"Because I know how your mind works, Gus." He grinned wryly. "You have something up your sleeve."

"Well…yes, I did have an idea. Why don't we go away for the weekend? I know ordinarily you wouldn't consider doing this, but these are both unusual cases that you can't do anything further with until Monday. I've already talked to Mrs. Bluefield. She can stay with Fritz."

"I suppose you've already made reservations as well."

"No, I wouldn't do that without making sure you agree to this." She caressed his face. "You know my Uncle Lenny wasn't able to come for our wedding because he was out of the country last spring. I'd really like to see him, and I haven't been to the Poconos in nearly three years. I checked on plane schedules. We could get an early direct flight to Newark, drive to Buck Hill Falls and be there in time for lunch. Then we can come back Sunday, leaving from Avoca Airport in Wilkes-Barre. It's closer but much smaller. However, there are flights out at eleven and four with a change in Pittsburgh. Whichever one you choose."

"Did the talk about your mother and the 1918 influenza epidemic have anything to do with this?"

"It may have. It certainly made me think about Lenny. He was so good to me when I stayed with him and my grandparents that fall and winter." She kissed him softly. "I'd like to show you that part of the country. It's beautiful. We can hike, take a boat ride, and just sightsee. A nice change for us."

He returned the kiss. "You know, it does sound good. Can you show me where you learned to shoot skeet?"

"Unfortunately, I can't. A dam was built in the mid-twenties to harness electric power, and a lot of land was flooded to create an artificial lake, covering even a small town. But it was a good move, and Lake Wallenpaupack is truly a beautiful lake."

"Yes, not surprising, since hydroelectric power is an important source of energy in this country. Okay, let's do it. I would like to see your Pocono Mountains."

"Oh, lovely. Do you want to fly back morning or afternoon?"

"Let's make it afternoon. Will we stay with Lenny?"

"No, I made a tentative reservation at a beautiful resort, Skytop Lodge. It's not far from Buck Hill. I'm sure you'll love it."

"I knew it, you did make reservations. Then we're definitely staying through the morning," Malcolm chuckled, pulling her closer. "You do manage to have all your ducks in a row, don't you, Mrs. Mitchell?"

"It's the result of scheduling all those rehearsals for shows and operas."

Augusta rested her head on his shoulder for a few minutes, enjoying the feeling of his warmth and strength.

She straightened and turned to gaze at him. "Mal— what Peter said to you about if the body is exhumed, this becoming a news story. Is there any way that could be avoided?"

"We will certainly try our best. And I'm sure the cemetery will cooperate as much as they can."

"I've been thinking about who might be in the casket. Do you think it's Wesley Vandergriff? There's quite a bit that points to his being the remains that were found."

"We also have a death certificate and grave site that indicate Vandergriff was buried in Spring Grove. As I told Peter, let's not get ahead of ourselves."

"Well, I have this theory." Augusta tucked her feet under her and knelt beside him on the sofa, eager to share her thoughts.

"Somehow I figured you would, Detective McKee-Mitchell."

"Oh, never mind." She turned away, a little annoyed.

Malcolm tipped her chin gently toward him. "No, I'd like to hear it. Just teasing."

"Here's the thing. You mentioned Jim had told you about all the problems with the civil authorities trying to figure out how to handle the situation…the situation with the flu, I mean. I read that article, too, and it sounded as if one day people were told one thing, and something else the next."

"Go on."

Augusta sat up straighter as she continued, "Well, the local authorities more than had their hands full. I have a difficult time imagining that Thomas Reichenbach could kill someone. Maybe accidentally, but not deliberately. But if he didn't, why were there bones under that patio? The only other person, or people, who could have buried them there would have been the masons."

"What does that have to do with the authorities having their hands full?"

"Don't you imagine there were a lot of crimes taking place at that time? People were out of work. Some of them were desperate. So, isn't it possible something could have happened with the masons that resulted in someone being killed? And if they wanted to dispose of a body, they had the perfect opportunity. Dr. Reichenbach wouldn't be around, he would never know."

"It's not impossible, but not likely. Don't forget, Jim talked to Herbert Bright and was told Dr. Reichenbach had called very early the morning they completed the work on the patio, and wanted it done immediately."

"Oh, I had forgotten about that. I suppose it would be easy to check on that company, too. Bright and Sons, to see if they had been engaged in any criminal activity."

"Jim did that. They had a clean record. Straight shooters."

"I just…Peter seems so upset about all this. I guess I'd like to try to prove his father wasn't involved. And his father's close friend, who still might be the victim until it's proven otherwise."

Mal gazed at her thoughtfully. "You know...I wonder just how close they were. Peter told you Wesley was often at their house, didn't he?"

"Yes. And I do wonder about this. If the body in Spring Grove is Wesley, how can you explain the pocket watch?"

"We don't have a positive I.D. on it."

"Do you really think Thomas Reichenbach might have killed his closest friend? People don't do that."

"It happens more often than you might think. And it generally is an impulse killing."

She had a sudden thought. "Have you ever asked Peter when the last time was that he saw Wesley?"

"I would like to ask him that. When we told Peter we thought we needed to exhume the body, he was pretty upset, so I didn't pursue it."

"Well...he was so young. And it was such a long time ago. He may not even remember. But if he did, he might remember how things were between his father and Wesley."

"All interesting speculation about puzzle pieces for a long-ago homicide, Gus. We may never find the pieces we would need to complete this one."

He leaned forward and kissed her again, his lips lingering on hers for a moment. "I'm taking Fritz for a nice long walk, and then I'd like to forget about all this for a while. Do you think you could help me with that?"

She kissed him for an even longer moment. "Indubitably, Detective Mitchell."

He grinned. "Meet you upstairs, Mrs. Mitchell."

Chapter 13
Stalled Cases

Thursday, November 4
7:00 a.m.

"You're up early." Malcolm had been awakened by the aroma of coffee, and when he went downstairs to be greeted by Fritz, he found Augusta seated at the table in the alcove, a legal pad in front of her as she made notes. He bent down and kissed her before pouring coffee for himself. "I take it Fritz has been walked."

"He has. And I am...up early." She stood. "What can I get you?"

"I'll get it. You're engrossed in something. Let me guess. Plans for the trip." He paused before going into the kitchen. "Have you eaten?"

"Yes, I had a croissant and a pear. And yes, I'm making a schedule for us."

Malcolm put bread in the toaster and took two pears from the refrigerator, peeling and slicing them. "You're excited about this, aren't you?" he called to her.

She came to the kitchen door. "Oh, I'm so pleased to have this chance to show you an important part of my childhood. You know, I spent part of every summer there until I finished high school."

Malcolm topped his toast with sliced swiss cheese and carried his breakfast into the alcove. As soon as he was seated Fritz was at his feet, gazing up at him and quivering in anticipation. "Yes, dog, I know you love cheese."

"Don't tease him, Mal. You know you'll give him some."

"Maybe. But he doesn't know that."

Augusta joined him at the table. "Do you have any idea how much I've loved your sharing with me the Cincinnati you grew up in? I know it's my city now, but I would never have explored places like Mt. Airy Forest by myself. And hearing your stories about attending Reds' games and then going to one with you. I even saw Fountain Square differently when you told me how excited you got as a little boy when your parents took you into town at Christmas to see the decorations." She leaned toward him.

"And I'm so happy you'll meet my uncle. You know how much I've loved spending time with your sister Amy and learning about her kid brother...the terrific little boy who was champion of the underdog, and came home more than once with a bloody nose after confronting a would-be bully. According to Amy, even then she figured you'd end up in law enforcement."

Seeing the sparkle in her eyes gave him a warm feeling, and he put an arm around her shoulders, leaned over and kissed her. "I hadn't thought of it that way. You're right, I haven't seen much of what you experienced when you were young. A brief visit to Philadelphia, but that was mostly to historical sites. I'm definitely looking forward to meeting the legendary Leonard Paynter, world traveler and man of many accomplishments."

Fritz whimpered and Mal held up a small piece of cheese. "Is this what you want?"

The puppy's tail thumped on the floor and he opened his mouth wide as he whined, making Mal and Augusta laugh. Mal dropped the cheese and Fritz, unblinking, caught it and swallowed it.

Augusta scratched his ears. "Did you even *taste* it?" she laughed.

"Sure you want to spend a weekend away from your baby?" Mal teased.

"Oh, I'll miss him. But he'll be here when we get back. And he won't miss school, Henrietta is taking him to his obedience class."

Malcolm swallowed the last of his coffee. "Will I see you later, or do you have to be at the Conservatory early?"

"I don't have to be there until six-thirty. I can fix a casserole so if you aren't home by six, you can just heat it for dinner."

"No, that's okay. Don't worry about it, I'll pick something up. *In bocca al lupo*, just in case I don't see you before you leave." Malcolm was proud to use the traditional operatic "good luck" wish: "In the mouth of the wolf."

She walked with him to door, responding "*Crepi il lupo* (may the wolf die)," before she kissed him goodbye.

***

Homicide Squad Commander Lt. Ray Kramer greeted Malcolm as he entered Detective Headquarters at City Hall. "I got the coroner's report on your bones, Mitchell," he said.

"Did you get the word from Jim about Peter Reichenbach asking us to wait on exhuming the body in Spring Grove?"

"Yes. He does understand our asking him was a courtesy? And that he has no legal means of delaying the exhumation?"

"Yes, he's aware of that."

"Then I'm inclined to contact the cemetery on Monday, regardless. I'd like to get this wrapped up as soon as possible." He frowned, and Malcolm had an idea there was a veiled reference to the Martin case in his comment. He was well aware how much his boss wanted that case closed. It had been hanging far too long.

Jim handed him coffee as Malcolm sat down at his desk. "I'm beat! I'm even looking at newspaper articles for clues about the Martin case."

"So, you know there's really not much in them. All the information came from us. You won't even find Walls mentioned…or the fatal shot behind the ear. Walls is just referred to as something like 'the prisoner' or 'the convict.' We wanted him to know we knew, but we didn't want any *Morning Call* reporters talking to him and mucking up the case. Which of course was correct. There's never been anything to directly connect him with the case, because Jesse won't talk."

"Have *you* interviewed Walter Walls?"

"Yeah, once. He has kind of a weaselly charm. He's got 'Who, me?' down to an art." Mal's phone rang. "Mitchell."

"Detective, there's a lady here who would like to see you if you have time. A Mrs. Reichenbach."

"Thanks, I'll come out."

Jim lifted an eyebrow.

"Mary Ellen Reichenbach wants to talk to me," Mal told him." Stay on the Martin case, will you? Maybe you'll be struck by something that will crack it wide open. Lord knows I've been over it a hundred times. On paper and in my dreams."

Malcolm noticed immediately that Mary Ellen seemed on edge. He led her to a conference room so they would have privacy. "Can I get you anything? Coffee? Pop? Iced tea?"

"No, thank you, Malcolm. I'm fine." She glanced nervously about the room. "I'm sure you never expected to see me here."

"What can I do for you, Mrs. Reichenbach?" Mal hoped his facial expression was one of helpful concern and would encourage her to speak openly to him.

"Well…I'm concerned about Peter. He's quite distressed about this whole situation, since you told him the…the remains that were discovered might be Wesley Vandergriff. In fact, he's convinced you believe they are."

"It certainly seems likely, but we need to exhume the body in Spring Grove before we can know that. I noticed Peter seemed agitated when I talked to him on Monday about this."

Mary Ellen leaned forward, clasping her hands on the table. "At first, he seemed to be taking it pretty well."

Malcolm nodded. "We've appreciated his cooperation."

"But for the past two nights, he's barely slept. He gets up after tossing and turning for an hour or so, then tiptoes out of the room to avoid waking me. When I've checked on him, I've found him in the living room or in the library. Mostly staring out of a window."

"Has he talked to you?"

"Not much. He just says, 'This is wrong. The dead should be left in peace.' He seems…he seems afraid of what you'll find when you open the coffin." She covered her mouth with her hands for a moment before continuing. "Maybe he's right. Whatever happened, it was nearly fifty years ago. Does it really matter?"

"It may have been a half-century since the victim we uncovered died, but there's no statute of limitations on murder. And it is clear this was not an accident. Another thing, the killer may not have been his dad. It may be someone still alive. We have to run down all the clues until there are none left to run down."

"So, there's no way you can stop the exhumation?"

"I'm sorry to say there is not. I learned today my superiors plan to begin the exhumation process on Monday. Peter can file an appeal, or file for an injunction from another court of record, but realistically, that's just delaying the inevitable. He has no standing in appeal or in any injunction because he is not next of kin or any kin. The longer he delays it, if he succeeds in delaying it, is just more nights staring out windows."

Mary Ellen looked down at her clasped hands. "I see."

"I *am* sorry, Mary Ellen. I hope Peter will be able to understand this has to happen. One thing I can tell you, though: I know he was concerned about there being publicity because of the exhumation. That isn't likely to happen. It will be done privately, when there is nothing else happening in the cemetery. Jim and I will have to be there, but we'll be as inconspicuous as possible. When the coffin is lifted, it will quickly be put into a waiting vehicle—possibly an ambulance—and transported to the morgue."

"Well, at least that is reassuring. I'll pass that on to Peter." She stood. "Thank you for talking to me, Malcolm." He helped her with her coat. "Are you attending Augusta's opera tomorrow night? Peter and I have tickets. Maybe by then he'll have settled down."

"Yes. I'll look for you at intermission."

Jim looked up when Mal returned to his desk, lifting an eyebrow.

"Peter's more upset about the exhumation than we realized. His wife says he hasn't been sleeping. Hopefully, I gave her some information that will calm him down—about how private the exhumation will be."

"Odd, how he seemed eager to cooperate with us at first, and now this," Jim remarked.

"Well, it's very personal. His father taking a life, especially the life of a man Peter considered one of the family."

He paused for a moment. "The other thing is, what was happening when this took place. How confusing and frightening the influenza epidemic must have been for children—an epidemic that took his mother from him. Hard enough for adults to deal with. All of this I'm sure has awakened some unwelcome memories."

"True. I wasn't thinking of all that."

Mal indicated the file on Jim's desk. "Any progress?"

"Nope, but I enjoyed reading this article. A little ray of sunshine in a dark time."

"About the puppy?"

Jim grinned as he lifted the article. "'Mrs. Gail Martin, widow of slain Patrolman Don Martin, and now the secretary of Detective Chief Harry Sandman, had City Hall in a bit of an uproar last week. One of the detectives gave her a puppy when she came to work one day and the frisky little canine kept escaping from its box and romping through the corridors and into offices despite the best efforts of Mrs. Martin and Colonel

Sandman. And it wasn't housebroken either.' I'd love to have seen that."

"I was here that day. It was a riot. He was a cute little guy, to be sure," Malcolm laughed. "I should have brought Fritz to work with me when Augusta and I were working on housebreaking him. Just think, all these experienced cops could have helped us with that."

Both men laughed. "Not nearly as entertaining, but another article, along with what I saw in someone's notes, had information I wasn't aware of about Frank Murph—one of the original suspects in Don Martin's death," Jim said. "He was killed in Indiana in August of this year. An altercation with a police officer in Fort Wayne. The article includes information about the Martin murder and says, 'Both Murph and his brother, Leonard Murph, were among dozens of suspects in the slaying. Leonard Murph was cleared after taking a lie test, but no test was even given to Frank Murph.'"

"Yes, but it was learned Frank Murph was in jail at the time Don Martin was murdered. That's why he was eliminated." Malcolm slammed his hands down on the desk. "Jim, we *know* who killed Don Martin. It was Walter Walls. He even bragged about it. Of course, he recanted when we talked to him: 'just bravado.' Bravado my butt! The only person who knows for sure is Jesse Walls, because he was there. And he won't talk. He'd fry along with his brother as an accomplice."

"And Walls' wife Anna won't say a word. She's frightened out of her wits of the man."

"We know that. We *all* know it." Malcolm linked his hands behind his head and leaned back in his chair.

"You know what—I think I'd rather face a half-dozen bad guys in a shootout than deal with a case we can't close, especially when we know we have the answers."

Jim lifted an eyebrow. "That's a little extreme, partner."

Mal sighed. "Yeah, it is. And Augusta would *not* like to hear me say something like that. Well, it's probably a good thing we're going away this weekend."

"Nice. You and Augusta are actually getting out of Dodge?"

"Definitely. She wants to show me some scenes from her childhood. She spent a lot of time in the Pocono Mountains in Pennsylvania when she was young. Her grandparents had a summer place there, and she has an uncle who still lives there. We're leaving early Saturday morning."

"What about Fritz?"

"Mrs. Bluefield is playing dog sitter for the weekend. They adore each other. Fritz watches TV with her. The lady loves soap operas."

Jim grinned. "No soap episodes on the weekend."

"Well, they'll find shows they both like. 'Lassie,' for sure; Fritz loves that one." Mal sat forward and reached for the items Jim had just been through. "Anyhow, I'm looking forward to the break."

Chapter 14
A Weekend of
Music and Memories

Friday, November 5
4:00 p.m.

Opening night of *Savitri* had gone well, exceeding Augusta's expectations. Her cast was in top form and the audience seemed captivated.

One more performance and then…we're off to the Poconos!

Augusta glanced at the clock as she put final items in her suitcase. "Mrs. Bluefield will be here at six. Do you want to just take our bags with us, or should we come back here after the opera performance?"

She and Mal had agreed to stay overnight at a hotel near the airport rather than at home for two reasons: Mrs. Bluefield, who was spending the night, wouldn't be disturbed by their rising early to catch their seven a.m.

flight, and they agreed it would probably be less disruptive for Fritz as well.

"Why come back here? We should just drive on over to the Holiday Inn, don't you think?" He eyed his wife appreciatively. "You look great. That's some outfit."

Augusta turned around slowly, showing off her forest green wool blend dress with a pencil skirt and round neckline, decorated by a double strand of pearls. A long, belted jacket and an ivory chiffon scarf would turn it into a perfect suit for travel. "I try to shop smart," she chuckled.

"You packed slacks, I guess." Mal stuffed boots and a pair of jeans into a duffel bag. Augusta had promised him a hike, even though their visit would be brief. Since it was November, taking a boat out on the lake at Skytop Lodge might not be possible.

"Of course, I did. And hiking boots." She flicked a tiny piece of lint from her neckline. "Well—I suppose you're right about heading on over to the airport. I just thought maybe we should check in on Fritz and make sure Mrs. Bluefield has everything she needs."

Mal put his arms around her. "Mrs. Bluefield is quite capable of picking anything up you may have forgotten. Fritz is going to be fine. You'll miss him a lot more than he'll miss us." He smiled as he gazed into her eyes. "Fritz and Mrs. Bluefield are buddies, Gus. Relax."

"I know you think I'm being silly. He's just a dog, after all."

"No, he's your baby. I get that. And he's not 'just a dog.' He's the greatest dog ever."

Augusta laughed and kissed him. "You're as bad as I am. You just won't admit it."

Milly and Garrett arrived at the Conservatory at the same time they did, and they walked into the building together.

"Want me to stop by your house while you're away to be sure everything is copacetic?" Milly mischievously asked her friend.

"Oh, for heaven's sake. You're as bad as Malcolm. I know everything will be fine. Am I acting like a Nervous Nelly or something? Mrs. Bluefield is fabulous. Fritz adores her. He won't even notice that we're gone."

"Good. Just concentrate on having a nice weekend together. But I'm only a phone call away."

Augusta went backstage to check on her cast, and found them vocalizing, completing their makeup, chatting, and drinking tea with lemon. "Just do exactly what you did last night. Stay on your toes, though. There's always a danger of second-night overconfidence. Though I'm sure that won't happen."

"We've got this, Professor McKee," Nando told her. "On the other hand, we managed to do okay last night and avoid opening night jitters. One of these days I'm going to be in a production that has more than two or three performances. Wonder what that's like?"

"I think you'll find out, Nando. By the way, the house is sold out tonight."

Remarks from the group: "Oh, that's great." "That's exciting." "Sold out? Didn't expect that."

"Will you be at the after party?" Arthur asked.

"Thank you for inviting me, but my husband and I are leaving right after the performance. We have an early flight out for a weekend away and are staying at the airport hotel tonight."

Various comments, giggles, and raised eyebrows caused Augusta to laugh. "Well, believe it or not, I *do* have a life, ladies and gentlemen."

Laughter and more chatter from the group. Augusta held up a hand. "*In bocca al lupo*, everyone. Have a fine performance." A chorus of voices responded, *"Crepi il lupo."*

She joined Mal, Milly, and Garrett in seats near the rear of the auditorium. The lights dimmed.

This was a favorite moment for Augusta. Near the end of the rehearsal process, she made a point of telling her cast that it was time for them to take ownership of the production. It was, after all, their show. By the first dress rehearsal—sometimes sooner—it unfailingly happened, and once she was sure all technical aspects were well in hand, Augusta relaxed and became an audience member. Undoubtedly, she was the most appreciative member seated in the audience, because she was so aware of all the hard work that had gone into this production. Watching the ease and confidence with which the cast performed thrilled her.

Difficult shows she viewed as something of a mine field, and the challenges in this one were apparent from the beginning. No overture of any kind, and the single, unaccompanied solo voice of Nando as Death had to immediately capture the audience's attention and set the mood. As soon as the shadow grew on the scrim, the audience quieted, and Nando's powerful voice filled the room as he sang: "Savitri! Savitri! I am Death!"

Augusta wasn't disappointed. Her cast enthralled the audience and performed expertly. There were even some exceptional moments—soaring, secure high notes from Savitri and Satyavan; exceptionally lovely sounds from the women's ensemble and the small orchestra; dramatic proclamations from Death—and a standing ovation once the opera was complete.

Mal wrapped an arm around her waist. "Well done, Augusta. I mean that."

"You liked it?"

"Well…I liked what I witnessed tonight. You put up an impressive production." He grinned. "However, I doubt there are fairies dancing around on Fountain Square."

She pressed her face against his shoulder to muffle her laughter.

"Here are the Reichenbachs," Mal warned.

Augusta turned to see Peter and Mary Ellen waiting to speak with her.

"So well done, Augusta," Mary Ellen said. "Some wonderful moments. What an interesting piece. Your cast was outstanding."

"Yes, it was challenging, Mary Ellen. Thank you so much for coming. I'll pass on your compliments to the cast."

Peter was silent for a moment, staring hard at Augusta and ignoring Malcolm.

What's going on with him? She glanced at Mal and saw the slightly lifted eyebrow.

"Why did you choose that opera, Augusta?" Peter asked.

"I didn't. John Edmanston selected the program and invited me to direct the Holst opera. It was a different experience, and I knew we had the singers to handle the demanding solo music."

"I see." He took Mary Ellen's arm abruptly. "We should get going. We're meeting friends for drinks."

On the drive to the airport hotel, Augusta observed, "Peter's behavior was bizarre."

"This whole situation with the bones being discovered and the possible ramifications are finally getting to him. I believe more than I realized."

"Maybe he'll be in a better place after the weekend, Mal. There's not a thing you can do about his state of mind, you know."

"I'm sure he wishes none of this had happened. But it did, and the mystery continues to unfold. I guess we could blame Fritz."

"For what, reacting like a puppy to earth being uncovered and all the magical discoveries that opened up for him? No, if anything Fritzy should be thanked for unearthing a secret that needed to be exposed."

"Remind me to thank the little guy when we get home." Mal stretched his arm behind Augusta's shoulders and pulled her closer. "A night out in a hotel. I think I'll focus on that."

"We have to get up at five, remember. And it's already after eleven."

He grinned as he glanced at her. "We can sleep on the plane."

***

Mal spotted Leonard Paynter before Augusta did as he strode briskly toward them in the airport lobby. *He could be her brother*, Mal thought. *The same youthful demeanor. At least six-two, about 165, the same eyes, graying hair that was once a reddish-brown. I'd guess his age at fifty-five rather than sixty-seven.*

"Here's Lenny, I think."

Augusta ran to embrace him, Mal right behind her.

"Hi, Malcolm. I'm Len." A firm handshake and steady gaze. *I like this guy already.*

"Great to meet you, Len. I know it's trite but I'll say it anyway: I've heard a lot about you."

"Let's collect your bags and get out of here. I hate the Newark Airport." Soon they were headed west in Len's roomy Lincoln Continental, the men in front and Augusta in the back.

"Nice car. 1965?" Mal asked.

"Yes, just picked it up a couple of weeks ago. How do you like the color, Augusta?"

"Pretty. What's it called?" She leaned forward.

"Madison Gray. A fancy name for blue gray."

Augusta leaned forward, her elbows on the back of the front seat. "Mal…maybe we need to get a new car. I really like this one."

"I thought the Imperial was your favorite, Gus. And the one we have isn't much over two years old."

Len guffawed. "Gus! Love it. How do you get away with that, Mal?"

"It just popped out one day, not long after we met. She gave me permission to use it."

The three laughed together. "Don't get any ideas, Lenny," Augusta remarked. "It's Malcolm's nickname for me. No one else calls me Gus."

Len glanced back at her. "Anybody ever call you Augie these days?"

Now it was Mal's turn to laugh. "Augie? Really?"

"I used to tease her with that nickname. She really, really hated it."

"She still does," Augusta chuckled. "Don't even think about using it again."

The road west took them out of the city of Newark and into pleasant countryside and occasional attractive small towns.

"Augusta told me about your dog unearthing human remains which appear to have been deliberately hidden in 1918. During the influenza pandemic."

"Surprisingly, we may even have identified them. We'll know sometime next week."

"Augusta and I spent a lot of time together that fall and winter. Philadelphia was one of the worst hit cities in the country, and her father asked me to bring her to the Poconos until it had died down. It was hard to leave my sister who had just become ill, but it had to be done."

The road began to curve more as the landscape became hillier. "I don't remember much about that," Augusta said. "I liked being with you and my grandparents. You kept me busy and tried to keep my mind off of anything sad or frightening."

"How severely was the Pocono area affected by the Spanish flu?" Mal asked.

"The area was sparsely populated, so it wasn't as bad as in a city. But it still created a lot of problems. Everything was shut down, but the flu continued to spread. There weren't many health care workers and eventually the small hospital was overwhelmed. Doctors and nurses were sent to Monroe County from other areas. Emergency hospitals were set up. The worst hit were Stroudsburg and East Stroudsburg, which were the population centers. And still are." Len eased to a stop at a traffic light.

"I'm still in my parents' home, which is away from that area and further up on the mountain. Oh, it's not really a mountain. The Poconos are tall hills. But there's a considerable difference in elevation."

"Gus told me about the Buck Hill house. You weren't near a town and she says the houses have a lot of land around them."

"Yes, so staying away from people wasn't a problem. We had a staff. A man and wife who looked after the house, cooked, and shopped. A gardener who wasn't very busy that fall once he'd cleaned up the leaves."

The road began to climb, winding through a dense forest. "This is beautiful," Mal remarked. "Such a variety of evergreens in this part of the country."

"We're going over Kittatinny Mountain. It's actually a ridge with a grandiose name, but it rises pretty high. The highest point in New Jersey."

"So, how did you keep Augie out of trouble?" Mal grinned at Augusta and she smacked his shoulder.

"We were outside as much as possible, but she wasn't allowed to leave our yard. We had a swing. And a lot of trees to climb. We played croquet and badminton, even though the weather was turning colder. We had a bow, arrows, and a target. And we snuck off a few times to visit the Buck Hill waterfall."

Mal turned to stare at Augusta. "You never told me you climbed trees when you were a kid."

"You never asked."

Len laughed heartily. "We played a lot of games in the evenings and when the weather was bad. Tons of card games. Backgammon. Checkers. But her favorite was chess."

"You never told me you play chess."

"You never asked."

They had passed through another small town and turned onto a bridge, stopping briefly to pay a toll.

"Delaware River," Len said. He pulled forward and turned right, heading north. "And now we're in Pennsylvania."

Mal noticed a looming shape ahead which he couldn't see well through the trees. "Is that Kittatinny Mountain? No, wait. Wrong side of the river."

As they drew closer Malcolm saw it was a steep cliff, rocky but with trees growing through the rock. A bend in the road, and a breathtaking vista unfolded. Malcolm now saw the rocky cliff loomed above them on the Pennsylvania side of the river, while an equally steep and rocky cliff stood to their right on the New Jersey side. The two cliffs looked as if they had somehow been hewn in half and were part of the same mountain.

Mal caught a sharp breath. "You sure didn't tell me about this."

"This is the Delaware Water Gap," Augusta told him. "I wanted to surprise you."

Mal craned his neck to see better as Len slowed the car. "I mean…Len, can we stop for a minute?"

"You've got it." He turned into a parking lot next to an elevated overlook. "To really see it you need to climb one of the hills. The one on this side is Mt. Minsi, and that's Mt. Tammany across the river. Next trip, maybe. But it's still pretty impressive."

Mal jumped from the car and ran up the steps, Augusta and Len right behind him.

"The is the Point of the Gap," Len said. "You can read about the geology on the historical marker. A spectacular sight about four million years in the making."

Mal stared across the river at the tall, rocky cliff, and behind him at its counterpart, tipping his head back to see better. "Climb the hills? Up those cliffs?"

Len chuckled. "Not unless you're a crazy person. No, there are trails on the other side. Not tough at all. Piece of cake for you."

"Yeah, I'm coming back. I'm going to climb both of these hills."

He turned to Augusta and before he could ask, she said, "Yes, I have. A number of times." She gazed into his eyes. "And I hoped you would say that. What I have planned for you on the rest of this trip isn't quite so awe-inspiring, but it's still lovely."

"And the river…it's so clear. So clean."

"This is what I miss most about this place when I look at the muddy Ohio."

Mal stared across the river again. "Holy…is that an eagle?"

Len gazed upward. "You have to look carefully. It could be a hawk."

He watched the bird flying in concentric circles, searching for prey. "Yes, definitely an eagle. See how its wings are spread out horizontally?"

"Yes, I see that."

"A hawk's wings are more of a V-shape."

Augusta and Len gave Mal a few more moments to drink in the scene.

"We should get going," Len said. "We still have about a forty-five-minute drive to Skytop." He headed for his car.

Mal pulled his wife close and kissed her. "I'm glad we came."

"Any special reason?"

"I'm beginning to get a picture of a spirited young girl I like very much."

"Oh, there's a lot more of her waiting to meet you," she laughed.

They sauntered back to the car, arms around each other.

Chapter 15
The Renaissance Man

The borough of Stroudsburg was much as Augusta remembered it. She pointed out the picturesque old courthouse and its surrounding square to Mal, and he commented on the tree-lined streets of the old town.

Continuing north, they came in sight of a long plateau, definitely higher than the surrounding hills. "Big Pocono Mountain. I think it might actually qualify as a mountain," Augusta commented. She leaned forward and peered at the hill. "Looks as if the ski area has been expanded considerably."

"It has," Len agreed. "Most people refer to this as 'Camelback' these days, and being able to create man-made snow has made a big difference."

They began to climb steadily, passed through more picturesque villages before pulling off the road at a small sign indicating "Skytop Lodge." A brief drive brought them to the front of the Main Lodge, a large Dutch Colonial-style manor house surrounded by spacious, well-groomed grounds, and overlooking a small, picturesque lake.

"Hmm. I guess 'elegant' is a good word? It's impressive," Malcolm remarked.

"It's everything a vacation resort should be," Len commented. "A nice choice of rooms of different sizes, all comfortable and quiet. Two excellent dining rooms, gift shops, a spacious lobby where good things happen. Activities offered to the guests if they're interested."

Mal laughed. "You sound a little like a promoter, Len."

"Well…it's the place I always recommend, even though there's another lovely old inn just down the road from my house. But there's no doubt Skytop has everything going for it."

Len helped carry their bags into the lobby. "I'll leave you two to enjoy the amenities. I'm cooking dinner tonight, by the way. We'll have more privacy and I'm a damned good cook." Mal and Augusta laughed.

"Why don't I pick you up at six? Augusta, will that give you enough time to accomplish whatever it is you have planned?"

"Six is perfect. And dinner at the house is even more perfect. Casual dress will be okay?" Len nodded and she gave him a warm hug.

He glanced at Mal. "You done good, kiddo. You couldn't have a better man."

"I agree. Wholeheartedly."

Len extended a hand to Malcolm. "Welcome to the family, Detective. I like seeing my niece so happy." He waved as he strode briskly out the door.

"Your Uncle Len is a pistol," Mal said as they unpacked. "Remind me again exactly what he did before he retired? Taught history somewhere, I think."

"Yes. He went to the University of Pennsylvania for his undergrad degree, then to Columbia for his first graduate degree. Then to Oxford for another degree in European history. He spent a little time traveling before he came home. He had a lot of offers, but decided to stay in this area since he had the house here and didn't care about salary—thanks to my grandparents, so he taught at Misericordia College, a Catholic school near Scranton."

"Then he retired about ten years ago and started traveling, right?"

"In between his travels he looks for ways to make a better world."

"Good luck with that."

"No, seriously. He works with different foundations that provide assistance for the poor. He's also an environmental activist. Soliciting donations, organizing fund-raising. But he does a lot more than that. He's hands-on. He works in soup kitchens. He gives free classes to college-age people who can't afford to go to college, and sometimes tutors them and helps them apply for scholarship assistance. Without them knowing it, at times that scholarship assistance comes from his own pocket."

"You're describing a kind of Renaissance Man. You know that, don't you?"

"Well, yes—that's how I see him. And he's also one of the smartest people I've ever known." Augusta closed the last dresser drawer and turned to Malcolm. "You know…what do you think about telling him more about the Vandergriff case? We're both so close to it. Maybe too close. Running it by someone who was around for the 1918 pandemic might give you a different sense of perspective. Len is aware of what the situation was in the U.S. at that time."

"I thought we were here to get away from that case for a while. Probably not a great idea."

"No, I guess you're right." She smiled. "Do you remember where Len was on our wedding day?"

"I think visiting a Buddhist monastery in Tibet, right?"

"Nepal. Luckily for us he's taking a little down time right now."

"Yes, I'm glad I have this chance to meet him." Malcolm pulled her down beside him on the bed. "So what's the game plan, bride?" He glanced around. "It's nice right here."

"I want to hike to a nearby waterfall. We need to get something to eat soon. Lenny's picking us up at six, and it's nearly noon. But you're right…it is nice right here."

She leaned against him briefly, but sat up abruptly. "Let's do this. I'll call the Tap Room and ask them to pack us a picnic lunch, and we'll hike to the falls and have our lunch there. It's not much more than a half hour away. Then after we come back, we can get cleaned up and rest for a while. After we have some 'us' time."

"I like the last part of your plan best."

"I want you to see the falls. They're beautiful. And there's only one other thing I want us to do in the morning."

"Another surprise?" He chuckled. "I guess it's in your genes. You're as indefatigable as Uncle Lenny."

"Time is precious. I don't like to waste too much of it."

They changed into hiking clothes and stopped at the Tap Room to pick up their food before striking out, heading north toward Indian Ladder Falls. Being in the crisp, clean air was invigorating, and they soon reached the falls. A slender upper cataract dropped from the hillside some fifty feet above them into a wider cataract which had two levels. A bench at the bottom of the falls provided the perfect picnic spot. They strolled back to the Lodge after eating, taking their time to enjoy the beauty and tranquility of the place.

The remainder of the afternoon went as planned. Mal held his wife in his arms as he relaxed against her. "Being with you…it's always new and exciting. And comforting. It's hard to remember what my life was like without you."

Augusta leaned up on one elbow and caressed his face. "I have to agree with my uncle. What he said about I couldn't have a better man in my life. I'm a lucky lady."

She kissed each of his eyes. "Let's get some sleep, my love. Lenny the dynamo has only two speeds: off and high."

Mal laughed, rested his face against her chest, and Augusta watched as he drifted off to sleep. *I love seeing him so relaxed. It means so much to me that I can do this for him.*

***

Len lived up to his boast of culinary prowess by providing a delicious meal of stuffed roasted Cornish game hens, mixed vegetables, salad, and an Irish cream-chocolate mousse for dessert. Augusta and Mal insisted on cleaning the kitchen, and finally, all three were comfortably ensconced before a roaring fire in the rustic living room, brandy in hand.

Len's color choices were reminiscent of Augusta's: soft greens and blues, with touches of more vivid color; chairs with ottomans and a deep, wide sofa. Oriental rugs adorned the floors. A gallery of photos over two walls: Len's many travels over the past years. One wall, floor to ceiling bookshelves crammed with books, a rolling ladder standing in front of it. The large stone fireplace took up much of the fourth wall. Photos of family were proudly displayed.

Augusta saw Mal's eyes sparkle when he spotted her as a child of twelve, shotgun in hand. "I love this. I wish I could have seen this young lady shoot. She tells me she was pretty good."

"She was indeed. Do you have her using a pistol yet?"

Mal laughed. "I'd like to, but she is one busy lady. And now that we have Fritz—our pup—she spends any spare time training him. And doting over him."

Len turned to Augusta. "How did your production of the Holst opera work out?"

"I think the audience appreciated what we did. I had a great cast. I doubt anyone will rush to buy a recording."

"I need to get back to India. And I also need to visit Pakistan."

Augusta sipped her Drambuie. "I will never understand how the British managed to subjugate an entire subcontinent."

"Very long story, my dear. I have some books I can lend you. And I agree, it's appalling."

Len swirled his brandy. "But I'd rather learn more about Malcolm and why he does what he does. Did you have law enforcement officers in your family?"

"No, I didn't. But my dad had a good friend who was murdered because two thugs wanted a car. When they were caught and incarcerated, my dad took me to Detective Headquarters to thank them." He grinned. "I guess I was pretty impressed. I knew then that's what I wanted to do."

"It's not an easy life, I'm sure. Augusta tells me along with the case of the unearthed bones, you're working on another. The recent murder of a fellow policeman."

"I am. It's been under investigation for over four years now. We're sure we know who the killer is. He's been in and out of jail most of his adult life. During his last stint, he even bragged about killing a cop. Of course, when confronted with that boast, he denied it. There were eyewitnesses but he was too far away for them to be able to positively identify him. And there was even another guy with him who won't give him up."

Mal gazed into the fire. "Knowing but not being able to prove that Walter Walls murdered Don Martin has been a sword in the side of the entire detective squad."

"I'm sure." Len poured more brandy into Mal's snifter. "Difficult for all of you."

"Walls is evil. One of the worst criminals I've ever dealt with. He needs to be tried and convicted for Don Martin's murder and executed, which is the sentence in Ohio for killing a police officer."

"As it is in most states. Feels like an appropriate punishment for such a crime."

"Well, I'm sure you'll understand when I say there is no adequate punishment in this life for the brutal murder he committed. But if we can't nail him for this, if he goes back to prison for some lesser crime, at least he'll have no more victims. That's the most important part of the job, to protect the innocent."

"'Protect and serve'. You consider it your duty to save lives whenever you can."

"Of course, I do. Even a suspected criminal's life. I'd much rather put handcuffs on someone than send them off in a hearse."

"Don Martin—I assume he was a young man?"

"Still in his twenties. He'd served three tours in Korea before he joined the force."

"I've been thinking about Augusta's mother Eileen—my sister. She was thirty when she died. The 1918 influenza killed so many young people of that age. Twenties and thirties, people with such promise. Promises that were never fulfilled. I know Eileen was looking forward to having more children."

"I've wondered about that," Augusta said. "Of course, many died in the war as well. A generation of unfulfilled promise." She murmured, "Wesley Vandergriff."

"Augusta," Malcolm warned. She glanced toward him and saw the lifted brow.

"The bones have a name," Len commented. "Not to worry, Detective. I am the soul of discretion."

"I'm sorry, Mal," Augusta said contritely. "Obviously, I wasn't thinking."

"Your bride can be impulsive, Detective Mitchell."

"Don't I know it."

Len gazed through the amber liquid in his snifter. "Wesley Vandergriff. An intriguing name and one I recall from many years ago."

"Well…I can't confirm what you just guessed, Len. In strictest confidence, it is a possibility."

"You heard Vandergriff play? In Philadelphia?" August leaned forward eagerly.

"I did. When I was at Penn, he performed a recital in the Catholic cathedral. I was taking a music literature course and our professor required us to attend certain musical events. It was the fall of 1917. He was brilliant. A consummate performer, charismatic and dynamic. The kind of performer you never forget."

"Obviously," Augusta said. "I've been told he was on a trajectory to stardom."

"I'll agree with that. A striking person, physically. Tall and slim. I remember thinking all organists should look like that. You had no doubt he had total command of that enormous instrument. And he played an extremely difficult program." He chuckled. "You know that expression, 'pulling out all the stops'? Well, he did that. There were times I would swear the building shook."

Len glanced at the clock on the mantle. "It's getting late. I should probably take you back to the Lodge. But before I do, I want to make a toast." He lifted his snifter toward each of them. "To my musical niece and her remarkable law enforcement officer."

Augusta laughed. "We get that a lot— 'the diva and the detective.' People are surprised that we're so happy together because what we do is so different."

"I don't find it surprising at all. A law enforcement professional and a teacher. People who help make civilization work." He paused. "People who care."

***

After an elegant and filling breakfast provided by room service, Augusta dressed in slacks, a shirt and a heavy sweater, once again donning her boots. Mal followed suit. "Just one last Pocono surprise before we have to get ready to go," she told him.

Len was waiting for them in the lobby, also dressed appropriately for an outdoor activity, chatting with a staff member who apparently was to be their guide.

"Good morning. This is Charlie. Charlie, this is my family, Detective and Mrs. Mitchell."

"Morning, folks. It's a beautiful day today. Ready to go?" He ushered them to a waiting jeep with the Lodge logo on it.

A drive to a part of the grounds at a distance from the Lodge brought them to a wooden building. Augusta glanced at Mal, who returned her gaze, mystified.

"All is about to be revealed." She caught her breath in excitement.

Mal gazed at the sky, peering at a distant spot on the horizon. "Isn't that the Delaware Water Gap?"

"It is," Len replied. "Gorgeous day. Sometimes it's not visible from here."

They walked into the building, through a narrow room piled with boxes, and passed through a second door.

Mal's face broke into a grin. "No kidding. You shoot skeet here?"

"This is our Sporting Clays Course," Charlie announced proudly. "So, who's shooting this morning?"

"I am." Augusta drew on snug leather gloves and examined the shotguns laid out on a table before her, trying them for weight, lifting them to her shoulder to test the length from barrel to wrist, putting an eye to the gunsight. She made a selection and Charlie provided her with goggles and ear protection. She quickly loaded shells into the gun and stepped to the railing.

"You'll start with ten targets," Charlie told her, holding up a clay pigeon—a disc about four inches in diameter. "The first two will be launched from the same angle. After that there'll be releases from random angles. I won't release any of the targets except on your command."

Augusta glanced at the two men, who leaned back against the wall. Len was grinning from ear to ear, and Mal still looked as if he had a hard time believing she could actually do this.

She shouldered her gun, moving the barrel slowly from side to side, getting a feel for the gun and the space she'd be observing.

"Pull!" Careful sighting as she established a lead on the target. *Find the apex. Wait, wait—now!*

The clay disc blew apart in midair. Augusta was thrilled.

"You've still got it, girl!" Len pumped a fist as she turned to her men. Mal was staring at her with a huge smile, his eyes shining.

"You do know I haven't done this in years," she said modestly. "Probably a lucky shot." *No, it wasn't. That was a perfect shot.*

She had only one miss in the next nine.

***

An early lunch in the Tap Room, and then a drive north to Wilkes-Barre's Avoca Airport.

"It looks like there aren't as many trees on these mountains," Malcolm observed.

"This is coal country," Len told him. "Pennsylvania is a country rich in natural beauty, and bountiful in more ways than one. Agriculture in some areas, minerals in others. Coal, primarily, throughout the state and the entire Appalachian region. This area has been heavily mined, creating deforestation and a lot of other environmental problems. I could go on and on about this."

As they waited on the tarmac to board their plane, Augusta invited Len to visit them in Cincinnati for Christmas.

"I'd like that," he replied. "I think I can make it work. Will I get to see Milly? You know she's one of my favorite people."

"Of course you will," laughed Augusta.

"I know this was a long way to come for such a brief visit, but I'm so glad we did it," she said to Malcolm once they were airborne.

"I am, too. It was a nice break, and meeting Lenny made the trip well worth it. And watching you shoot skeet. You're damned good at it."

"Just lucky," she replied with a smile.

"Lucky my backside. You knew exactly what you were doing. It was pretty awesome to watch. Now you have to come to the shooting range and try a pistol. You're a natural, Gus."

"Why didn't you try shooting? I know it's different from what you have to do in police work, but I think you would have enjoyed it."

"First of all, it was your moment. Second of all, you're right, it's different. There's a rhythm to it. I saw what you were doing as you followed the pigeon. You had to anticipate where it would be and shoot ahead of it so your shot would get there at the exact same time. Hard to believe you only missed once after all these years. My own Annie Oakley."

Augusta gurgled with laughter. "It was so much fun. But you know what? My shoulder is going to be *so* sore tomorrow. There is a kick. If I'd tried ten more targets, I don't think I'd have done so well. My arm was already feeling it."

An easy change of planes in the spacious Pittsburgh airport, and a final short flight to Cincinnati.

When they collected their car, Augusta extended her hand for the keys. "Let me drive, Mal. I know you have a long day tomorrow."

He dropped them into her hand. "I am kind of tired. But it's a good tired. Thanks for playing chauffeur, Mrs. Mitchell."

"It's my pleasure, Detective. The least I can do since you let me drag you 1200 miles in forty-eight hours."

He relaxed in the passenger seat, leaned his head against the backrest and turned toward her. "I liked having the chance to meet Augie," he teased, and she smacked his thigh as they both laughed.

They drove up to their house just before eight, Fritz's excited barking greeting them as they approached the front door. Augusta knelt and hugged her puppy as he wagged his entire body, covering her face with doggy kisses.

"Everything go okay?" Mal asked Mrs. Bluefield, who appeared right behind Fritz.

"Yes, absolutely. And such perfect timing. We just finished watching 'Lassie.' Didn't we, Fritzer?"

She patted the dog's head. "I'll be out of your way in just a couple of minutes. I'm all packed and have my bag right here by the door."

"I'll get that for you," Mal offered.

"Oh…Detective Mitchell…your partner called. He asked me to give you the message that Mr. Reichenbach is planning to file some kind of legal document tomorrow. He said you'd understand."

Augusta glanced at Mal, who gave her a wry grin. "Back to reality."

Chapter 16
The Reichenbachs

Monday, November 8
7:00 a.m.

Mal picked up his private line in the alcove on the first ring. "Mitchell."

"Hi, Dad."

"Hey, Ryan. Nice to hear from you. What's up?" Malcolm seldom saw his busy elder son now that he was an attorney in a prestigious civil law firm.

"Well, good news and bad news. Here's the good news, and it's pretty great. I proposed to Lacey last night and she said yes."

Mal glanced at Augusta, giving her a big grin as she came in from a walk with Fritz. "That is great news, son. Congratulations."

"We'd love it if you and Augusta could celebrate with us soon. We're thinking a casual dinner at

Mecklenburg's on Friday, and I'll see if Danny and Martha can make it."

"Hang on a minute. Augusta just brought Fritz in from a walk. I'll check with her." He covered the mouthpiece with his hand and relayed the invitation.

"Of course! How exciting." Augusta took Fritz into the pantry to feed him.

"We're in. Just let me know what time. You said bad news? What's that about?"

"Peter Reichenbach. He showed up at the office late Friday afternoon and asked me to represent him. He wants to file a stay, or an injunction, or whatever legal action he can take to stop the exhumation of a body in Spring Grove Cemetery. He says he isn't a relative of the man who is interred, so I advised him he doesn't have much chance of stopping it. I also told him I wouldn't be able to represent him, in any event."

"He asked for you, specifically?"

"Yes. I guess he thought because he knows you, I might have some clout. I explained the conflict of interest issue."

"Thanks, son. How much did he tell you?"

"A lot more than he should have. Listen, I'll get back to you with a time for Friday after I call Dan." Ryan chuckled. "How about that? The Mitchell men and our artistic ladies."

Augusta brought her breakfast of half a grapefruit and toast and joined Malcolm at the table, Fritz at her heels. "I'm thrilled for both of them. I knew Lacey was the right girl for Ryan the first time I met her."

"Why do women always say that?"

"Well, I did think so. Have I ever said that about any of the other females he's brought around the past two years?"

"I plead the Fifth." Malcolm grinned as she punched his arm.

"In fact, when I saw her portray Portia at Parkside Playhouse and noticed Ryan in the audience, I thought about playing matchmaker. That's how right for him I think she is."

"Well, you quickly learned that he was there as her guest." Malcolm reached down and scratched the pup's ears.

"Yes. And I thought, 'even better.' Isn't it interesting the women your sons have chosen to spend their lives with?"

"Women who have a lot in common with their stepmother, you mean."

"I didn't say that, did I? Smart, talented, strong, caring, lovely, terrific young women."

"Just like their stepmother." He leaned over and kissed her. "Well, you may not have played matchmaker for Ryan and Lacey, but you sure did for Danny and Martha."

"No, I didn't. I just happened to be there when they met. You were there, too. You must have noticed that spark between them."

"I did. Maybe not love at first sight, but something pretty close. Stay, Fritz." Malcolm took his dishes into the kitchen, washed them and put them away. "I have to get going. Peter Reichenbach notwithstanding, that exhumation will take place sometime this week."

"I'll look forward to seeing Ryan and Dan on Friday."

"I will, too. Do you have lessons this morning?"

"Not until ten. I'll walk Fritz again before I leave. He's doing much better about being left alone."

"So you said before the infamous feather incident."

"Well, he is. Aren't you, Fritzy?"

Fritz's eyes brightened and his tail thumped on the floor.

"Remember to turn on the TV for him." Malcolm patted the dog's flanks. "He likes listening to the '50/50 Club.'"

"I know he does. Just like Caruso did." She gazed at Fritz fondly as he looked from one of them to the other, lifting his ears.

Malcolm burst out laughing. "Are we sappy or what?"

Augusta stood and wrapped her arms around him. "It was a good weekend, wasn't it?"

"The best." He kissed her, lingering a moment.

She pulled back. "Get going, Detective. But hold that thought."

***

Augusta stopped in the office at around three before she left the Conservatory. Anne Evans, Dean Williamson's secretary, smiled up at her.

"Anne, I'm running down to *The Morning Call* to pick something up, and thought I'd offer my services as a messenger if you have anything you'd like handed to someone on the staff. I know mailing items down there isn't always the best way to be sure they're delivered properly."

"Oh, you're a doll, Augusta." Anne fished a file from a stack on her desk. "This is a press release about registration for next semester for the preparatory students. If you could hand it to the education editor, I'll buy you lunch."

"No need, I'm happy to help you with this." *Oh, good. Now I have a legit reason for being there.*

Her mission was to try to find any old photos of Wesley Vandergriff in the archives. Augusta's talks with Nathan Fischer and Titus Powlett had intrigued her, and she'd like to see this man who apparently was as charismatic as he was gifted.

She was sure one of the staff reporters, Arnold Richter, would help her. Augusta did not like or trust Arnold Richter, but they maintained a cordial truce, and she asked for him when she arrived at the reception desk.

Arnie appeared quickly after the receptionist relayed her message, and Augusta noted what she thought of as his rather self-important little swagger as he walked toward her. While Arnold Richter was tall, he was anything but dark and handsome, with sandy, thinning hair and pale eyes. His usual facial expression was one twitch away from a sneer.

"Well, well, well. Are you here as Professor McKee or Mrs. Mitchell?" He smirked.

"Professor Mckee," she said, sweetly. "I have a press release from the Conservatory for the education editor, and I know you'll be sure it gets on her desk."

He took the file from her. "Done. Anything else?"

"Yes, I have a friend who is planning to write a biography of a musician who achieved some fame locally—and nationally—decades ago. An organist. Have you ever heard of Wesley Vandergriff?"

"No, I don't believe I've ever heard that name. An organist? As in a church organist?"

"That was how he began, but he gained some prominence as a concert organist in the early decades of this century. My friend tells me he had great promise and it was thought he might have an international career that would have rivaled E. Power Biggs."

"Now, him I *have* heard of. What was the man's name? Wesley something?"

"Wesley Vandergriff. Tragically, he passed away around 1920 before his promise came to fruition. Anyway, my friend knew I planned to stop by the paper, and asked if I would see if there might possibly be any photos of Vandergriff in the archives."

"We can check together if you have some time," he offered, rather condescendingly.

How kind you are. Easy, Augusta. Don't let him hear the sarcasm. "I have about an hour. Is that long enough?"

"Probably. What years should we look into?"

"This was a very long time ago. I'd say between 1910 and 1920."

"I doubt there are many, if we have them at all. But let's give it a try."

Augusta followed him into a large room filled with filing cabinets. He looked first by name with no luck, then he tried by subject matter and year, looking through a drawer marked "Musical Events 1910-1920," again checking by name.

"Here he is. Yes, there are three articles with photos."

They moved to a desk where Arnold removed each item, carefully placed in a glassine envelope. Augusta sat at the table to look them over. The first was an article dated March, 1916, about Wesley performing a series of concerts in nearby cities. The photo with the article was a head shot, professionally photographed. A man with a longish face, quite attractive, twinkling eyes. As was the practice at the time, he wasn't smiling, but it appeared he had to work hard not to. Smile lines framed his mouth, and his eyes had a definite twinkle to them. Wavy dark hair.

The second included a photo of Wesley and Titus, which surprised her, since Titus hadn't made mention of it. Wesley had won a competition and was pictured with his teacher accepting an envelope which the article indicated contained a check. The date indicated January, 1917.

The third Augusta studied for several minutes. Wesley standing next to an organ console with two women beside him, October, 1917. The ladies had been instrumental in raising funds for a new organ for a church in Hyde Park, and the article announced the dedication recital.

The woman nearest Wesley was identified as Mrs. Thomas Reichenbach. Petite, with a softly pretty face, large eyes and fair hair. Her face was tipped up as she gazed at Wesley. Vandergriff returned the gaze.

I'd love to get a closer look at this. I think this might be more than a "patroness-musician" relationship.

"These are wonderful. I know they would be a big help to my friend. Is there any way I could get copies?"

"Well…generally there is a fee, but I can give you copies of these as a courtesy. But if the author wants to use them, she'll need to apply for permission, and in that case, she'll be charged."

"That's fine, I'll pass that on. I'll wait if you have time to copy them now."

***

As often happened, Mal didn't get home until late. Augusta knew better than to ask why, but she reheated lasagna for him and sat with him as he ate, saying little but letting him know she was there if he needed to talk.

He pushed the plate back and sighed. "That was delicious, Gus. Thanks."

"I'm glad it helped."

"Jim and I were called in on a domestic dispute that turned into a hostage situation. Thank God nobody was hurt, but it was touch and go."

He stood and stretched. "I'll take Fritz for a walk. It'll help me unwind."

Augusta went upstairs and placed the articles she'd picked up at *The Morning Call* on her dresser. *Mal needs to see these.*

She was in her robe brushing her hair when Malcolm came into the room. He removed shoes and jacket, put his gun away in the top drawer of the chiffonnier, and relaxed in a chair.

He gazed at her for a moment. "Thanks again, Mrs. Mitchell. For the food, and for understanding I needed to decompress."

"Of course. You've told me domestic situations can escalate very quickly and become very bad. I'm grateful that didn't happen this time—partly, I'm sure, because of my brilliant husband."

He grinned. "It was a pretty full day, that's for sure. I spent some time earlier learning quite a bit about Dr. Thomas Reichenbach. He was a really good person, Gus. If he were still alive, he'd be about eighty today. Peter told us he retired when he was sixty-five, and he died five years ago. We know he never remarried."

"What did you learn today? I take it you spoke with someone." Augusta piled pillows behind her and stretched out on the bed.

"Yes. I actually talked with two physicians who were contemporaries of Thomas Reichenbach. They had nothing but the highest praise for him, both as a doctor and as a human being. I learned some interesting stuff. I hadn't realized how primitive medicine was in this country until about the last two decades of the nineteenth century. Nor did I know that one big reason for the rapid advancement was the establishment of Johns Hopkins. First the university, and then the hospital, which is where Dr. Reichenbach trained."

"I wasn't aware of that. I know how respected both are, though. So, he came back home to Cincinnati with an exemplary education as a doctor."

Mal nodded. "He was a dedicated, caring doctor who was also an advocate for his patients. I found it interesting that his specialty was infectious disease—things like tuberculosis, pneumonia, influenza, and even malaria. When the pandemic hit, every physician in this entire country did whatever needed to be done. Twelve-hour days were the norm. Sometimes all hospital workers drew even longer shifts."

He gazed off into the distance and added softly, "And then he had to watch his wife die of that awful disease. I can't imagine what that did to him."

Augusta grew silent for a moment. "You said Peter told you he changed after Alice's death. And as you just said, he never remarried."

Mal shifted in the chair, resting his elbows on the arms. "He devoted himself to his medical practice. He was known to treat patients at no charge if they couldn't afford the fees, or sometimes even pay the hospital costs himself."

"In that respect, he reminds me of my Uncle Lenny."

"He also spent a lot of time in various medical research facilities, searching for answers to viral infections. The virus that caused the so-called Spanish flu wasn't actually identified until decades later." He paused. "Do you remember that outbreak in the winter of 1957?"

"The flu that came through that year? I definitely do. I had it. It was the sickest I've ever been in my life. It knocked me off my feet for a couple of weeks."

"You didn't get the vaccine that was available for that particular flu strain? You might have avoided it. It would at least have made your illness less severe."

"I don't recall why I didn't, but I missed my opportunity. I won't do that again, for sure."

"Well, Thomas Reichenbach was one of the physicians who helped develop that vaccine."

Augusta sat up and stared at him. "It's obvious Thomas Reichenbach doesn't fit the profile of a cold-blooded murderer. Anything but. Are you thinking what I am, that if he did kill who we suspect is Wesley Vandergriff, he didn't plan it? Do you believe it was a crime of passion?"

"At the moment I think that's the best explanation." Mal stretched out his legs and linked his fingers behind his head. "But what could have enraged him so that he'd kill his best friend?"

Augusta went to her dresser and picked up the copies of the newspaper articles. "I went to visit our friend Arnie Richter today at *The Morning Call*. After what I heard about Vandergriff from Nathan and Titus, and then from Len over the past weekend, I was curious to see if I could locate a photo of him. I told Arnold I had a friend who plans to write a book about Vandergriff and wondered if the newspaper had material on him."

"And which friend did you make up that information about? Milly?"

"Well, no, I didn't give him a name. But Mary Ellen Reichenbach is a writer."

Mal grinned. "You actually went to see Arnold? I guess you *were* curious to get a look at Wesley."

He studied the photos she handed him, pausing when he looked at the third—the picture that showed Alice Reichenbach and Wesley standing next to each other.

"Well…this is interesting."

"I thought so, too. Did Peter indicate there might have been more than friendship between his mother and his honorary uncle? Of course, he was very young, and it's likely he wouldn't have noticed anything. I'm sure if they were involved, they were very careful to hide it from her young son."

"Jim and I are scheduled to talk to Peter tomorrow morning. He left a message for us this afternoon, inviting us to come to his house. Kind of odd, because he has classes every day at one school or the other." Malcolm handed Augusta the newspaper articles.

"We need to find out why he suddenly has become so uncooperative, to the point of threatening legal action to block the exhumation," Mal remarked. "I have a feeling he doesn't want us to learn Wesley Vandergriff is not in that coffin in Spring Grove Cemetery. That he's fearful of learning it *was* Wesley buried behind the house."

Augusta replaced the articles on her dresser and slid into Malcolm's lap. "You can't do anything tonight, my love."

She began to unbutton his shirt. "Remember that thought I asked you to hold onto this morning?"

Malcolm gazed into her eyes and gave her the smile that melted her insides. "You bet I do."

Chapter 17
Pieces of a Puzzle

Tuesday, November 9
10:00 a.m.

"Peter doesn't have classes this morning?" Mal turned up the driveway to the Reichenbachs' home.

"Mary Ellen said he's taking a couple of days off. She sounded concerned, Mal. More than concerned. Distressed," Jim replied.

"Let's hope we can get to the bottom of this. When I saw him Friday at the opera workshop performance, his behavior bordered on bizarre."

Mary Ellen met them at the door. "He's in the library. It's…kind of his safe haven, you know."

"Thank you. Are you coming in with us?" Jim asked.

"Yes, I think I should. I want to hear what he has to say to you."

Malcolm recognized the music Peter had playing on the stereo. Rachmaninoff, *The Isle of the Dead*.

Well, that's an interesting choice. Wonder if Vandergriff ever adapted it for organ.

Peter, lost in thought, glanced up and waved them toward seats. Mal waited as the piece wafted through the room, creating an atmosphere of melancholy. Peter stared into the distance, looking as if he could see wraiths filtering through the windows.

Jim glanced at Mal, lifting an eyebrow, and Mal shook his head almost imperceptibly. Finally, the music built to a climax and drew to a close. Peter went to the stereo and turned it off.

"Powerful piece of music, don't you agree? It's entitled *The Isle of the Dead*," Peter told them as he returned to his seat. "Thanks for coming, Detectives." He gazed at Mal. "Do you know that piece?"

"I've heard it. Rachmaninoff. I prefer the piano concertos."

Peter leaned forward. "I asked you to come here so I could convince you not to exhume Wesley Vandergriff's body. I don't understand why it's necessary. Whatever happened that resulted in a skeleton being found in the backyard of my family home in Hyde Park, happened almost fifty years ago. My father may have been involved in some way. Wesley may have been involved in some way. Who knows? Maybe people saw the masons preparing to lay the patio and brought a body in during the night to hide it."

Jim cleared his throat. "Well, anything is possible."

"You see? Detective Edmonds agrees with me. It's ancient history. All of the parties have been dead for...years. Some for decades. I'm happy to pay for burial of the bones that were unearthed. Some poor John Doe who died at the hands of...maybe a robber."

Mal caught Peter off guard by asking, "Do you remember the last time you saw Wesley Vandergriff?"

"What?"

"Wesley Vandergriff. When was the last time you saw him? Was it at your house?"

"No, I don't remember. I have no idea when." He mopped his face with a handkerchief.

"What was his relationship with your father? You said they were best friends. How would you define that, exactly?" Mal spoke in a low, conversational tone, but Peter became increasingly agitated.

"I see this was a mistake." He stood abruptly. "I won't be grilled this way." His voice began to rise in pitch. "I'd like you to leave my home."

Clenching his hands, Peter sputtered at Mal, "This is all your damn dog's fault. Digging around in the neighbor's yard." He stalked from the room.

Mary Ellen pressed a hand to her mouth. "I'm so sorry, Detective Mitchell. He doesn't mean that, the bones were bound to be discovered when your neighbors decided to replace the patio. I can't reason with him. I wish I could be more helpful."

Mal inclined his head. "I'm sorry as well, Mrs. Reichenbach. It's unfortunate he's become so upset and uncooperative. Do you have any idea why? At first he was very helpful."

"I wish I knew. He isn't sleeping, you know. When I sense he's being more reasonable, I'll urge him to contact you."

Mal glanced into the living room on their way out, and spotted a painting above the mantle. "Wait…is that a portrait of Alice Reichenbach?"

"Yes. Would you like to look at it?"

"Please."

"This was painted the year before she died," Mary Ellen told them. "She was thirty-one, but I think she looks younger, don't you?"

Large, dark eyes, pale blond hair, a sweetness to her features. And Peter doesn't look at all like her, except for the dark eyes. "She certainly was a beautiful woman. Thank you for letting me admire her."

The men returned to their car, Mal again opting to drive.

"That went well," Jim said, and they both laughed ruefully.

***

Let's say there was a romantic triangle—Alice, Thomas, Wesley. I need to learn more about Alice in particular. And Wesley as well. I've heard a lot about him as a performer, but not much about his personal life. I think we have a good idea who Thomas was.

Mal decided a good starting point was their obituaries, and the best place to find those was the Hamilton County Public Library. The pride of both the city and the county, the library fronted on Vine Street and covered almost the entire block between Eighth and Ninth Streets. The contemporary design, spacious and airy, and the unusually large collection of materials drew hundreds of patrons daily. Mal went to the newspaper archives and placed his request with the staff member on duty. He found a space at a reading table.

REICHENBACH, Mrs. Thomas – it is with sorrow that we learn of the death of Alice Reichenbach, wife of Dr. Thomas Reichenbach. She died on Thursday, October 17, of the influenza and was laid to rest in Spring Grove Cemetery on Sunday, October 20. A lovely young woman of only thirty-two years who was beloved by all who knew her as a gracious soul and a beautiful singer, and a lady of exemplary Christian virtue. Deepest sympathy is extended to her bereaved parents, Mr. and Mrs. Alphonse Addleman, her young son Peter, aged ten, who adored his mother, and her grieving husband, a respected physician in this city. She will be greatly missed by all.

Alice was a singer. Wonder why no one has ever mentioned that? "Pleased to meet you, Alphonse Addleman," Mal murmured under his breath. "How did you treat your daughter?" *Did Alice and Wesley ever perform together? That would have given them an excuse to see each other, even after Alice and Thomas were married.*

Peter was ten when Alice died. Her only child. Unusual for that time, larger families were the norm. Thomas and Alice must have been married at least eleven years at the time of her death. On the other hand, Augusta had no siblings, though Len said Eileen hoped for more children.

Mal recalled Peter talking about hearing Wesley play something on the organ, so at times he must have gone with Alice if and when she rehearsed with Wesley. "But not every time." A library patron stared at him and put her finger to her lips and he mouthed, "sorry," not realizing he had spoken aloud.

> VANDERGRIFF, Wesley — noted musician and concert organist, Mr. Wesley Vandergriff died of the influenza in General Hospital on October 23, 1918 and was interred in Spring Grove Cemetery on October 28. He was much admired for his ability and his performance skills and had appeared in concerts throughout the Eastern states and also had been seen in Montreal and Toronto in recent times. He was considered a musician of great promise whose budding career was sadly cut short long before it should have been. He was only thirty-four years of age, another victim of the terrible influenza epidemic ravaging our shores. He will be mourned by a wide circle of friends and admirers.

Malcolm asked the librarian if he could have copies of the two obituaries, and she returned promptly with a file for him. He hesitated a moment before he left, wondering if he should also ask for Thomas' obituary, but decided he had more information already from the interviews with people who had known him. *How differently it would be worded, though. 1918 compared with 1960.*

Back at Detective Headquarters, he started a file marked "Vandergriff Case" and transferred the obituaries. He added Gary's findings and felt fairly confident the following day he'd receive confirmation that the body scheduled to be exhumed was not Wesley.

How did it happen? Alice was buried on October 20. A body in General Hospital was claimed as Wesley's body three days later. Mal jotted dates down on a pad.

"Jim, did your buddy Herbert Bright remember the date he and his dad completed work on the patio behind Thomas Reichenbach's house?"

"I can get in touch with him and find out. That's asking a lot, though, Mal. Forty-seven years ago? He remembered it was late October." Jim picked up the phone.

"Yeah, that's true. Well, it might be helpful if I have the date."

Jim grinned. "Putting some puzzle pieces together, are we?"

"Thinking about it."

He stared at what he'd written: Alice was buried on October 20. On October 23 a body was declared to be Wesley Vandergriff. *Thomas killed Wesley sometime between those two dates, I'm sure of it.*

What about Alice's funeral? Could Wesley have attended it? Not likely. I don't think things were as bad here as Garrett described them in Philadelphia, but I doubt anyone beyond immediate family would be allowed at the grave site.

Speculating, he considered a possible scenario: Not long after Alice was buried, Wesley came to the house to offer his condolences. It would have been at night, maybe late at night. If Wesley and Alice were having an affair, maybe Thomas somehow found out about it. Out of his mind with grief and anger, he stabbed Wesley and then…*and then what?*

Malcolm threw his pen down on his desk, running a hand through his hair. *This is all conjecture. I need more information.* The obituaries were a start, but he needed to talk to Titus.

***

Mal had offered to provide dinner and he stopped at Skyline Chili, a weekly happening in the McKee-Mitchell household. Augusta always thought of the first time they had eaten Skyline Chili together during the Linnea Murphy case, when Malcolm had told her why he became a homicide detective. It was also the first time he kissed her. *That* she would never forget.

Fritz was required to stay at a distance from the table, but as always, he watched every bite they took, following the forks from plate to mouth.

"Is he watching you or me?" Mal asked.

"He's trying to watch both of us," Augusta laughed. "Hoping for a bite to drop to the floor."

"It's never happened."

"As far as he's concerned, that doesn't mean a thing. Hope springs eternal."

She added more oyster crackers to her three-way, chili with spaghetti and cheese. "Your encounter with Peter Reichenbach certainly does sound odd. Like he's hiding something."

"We thought the same. Well, the exhumation is scheduled for tomorrow afternoon, and it's going to take place, regardless of Peter Reichenbach's wishes."

He cut the spaghetti with knife and fork. "I want to find out more about Wesley Vandergriff. I went to the library today and found Wesley's obituary, as well as Alice Reichenbach's. There's not a lot of information in them. I made an appointment to talk to Titus Powlett tomorrow morning. He may be our best source. The only other items we have at the moment are the newspaper articles your buddy Arnie found."

The house line rang and Augusta picked it up. "Hello?"

"Hi, Augusta. This is Peggy Worthington."

"Hi, Peggy. What's up?"

"Do you know a reporter from *The Cincinnati Morning Call* named Arnold Richter?"

Augusta motioned to Malcolm to sit closer as she repositioned the handset so he could hear the conversation. She mouthed "Arnold Richter" and Mal nodded.

"Yes, I do. Why do you ask?"

"Well, he was here this afternoon, asking a ton of questions. Somehow, he'd heard the coroner was here last week, and he'd found out there were bones in our backyard."

"Oh, dear. I'm sorry to hear that."

"I think Charlie handled it perfectly, though. He told Mr. Richter that yes, indeed, we were having our patio replaced, and when the old flagstones were removed remnants of bones were found under them."

Mal did a thumbs up.

"Well said, and true," Augusta replied.

"Charlie told him the coroner took the bones to his lab and it's our understanding they proved to be ancient. Probably from a Native American burial ground."

Augusta giggled. "Good for Charlie."

Malcolm motioned to her to hand him the phone.

"Peggy, please thank Charlie for handling that so well. I'm sure if Richter pursues this with the coroner, he'll be stonewalled."

Laughter on the other end of the phone.

"Did he give you any idea how he learned about the coroner being at your house?"

"No. But people love to talk. I doubt it was one of the neighbors but you never know. I suspect more likely someone who was in the neighborhood and saw the hearse. Maybe a delivery person, maybe someone doing yard work."

"You're probably right," Mal said. "If he comes by again send him down here."

"Are you sure? You don't need that."

"Oh, Mr. Richter and I have an ongoing uncordial relationship."

Peggy laughed again.

"Anyway, thanks for letting us know. Sorry you had to deal with that." Mal hung up the phone. "Arnie strikes again."

Augusta stood and gathered their plates and cutlery as Fritz jumped up, tail wagging hopefully.

"He may be appeased for now…but I doubt that's the end of his snooping."

"As you like to say, Gus, 'he's just doing his job.'" Mal and Fritz followed her into the kitchen.

"Maybe it's time for Arnie to find another job." She ran water into the sink. "Wonder if the *Timbuktu Times* is hiring?"

Chapter 18
Guinevere

Wednesday, November 10
7:30 a.m.

"I'd really like to be in on this." Augusta had listened raptly to Mal's recent speculations about Wesley Vandergriff and Alice Reichenbach, and was intensely curious about what information Titus Powlett might provide.

"You have lessons. And I think a Music Lit class? This is your day at Cliffside, correct?"

"I could take a personal day. Mal, Titus knows me. I think he'll be much more comfortable if I'm there. I've worked with you before."

"Yes, but during informal meetings when I'm not on the clock. This is an official interview for a homicide case. You know I can't include you under these circumstances." He stood. "Besides, he may not be able to tell me much of anything. I have no idea if he even knew Thomas Reichenbach and Alice Addleman."

"I wish I had thought to ask him more when I saw him last week." Augusta crossed her arms over her chest, pursed her lips and glared at the table.

"Don't pout, Gus." Malcolm grinned and tipped her chin up. "I'll take copious notes and tell you everything when I get home tonight. I promise."

Driving to City Hall, he wondered how well Titus Powlett had known Wesley Vandergriff. Powlett could be his best source of information about what Malcolm strongly suspected was a crime of passion, and a love triangle certainly could be a motive for just such a scenario.

Arriving at Detective Headquarters he found a gloomy Jim Edmonds waiting for him. "Bad news. Jesse Walls is still in the wind. And worse news. Anna Walls is apparently living at present with a relative in Michigan. Trying to tie up the Don Martin case is looking like a pretty dim prospect."

"We can hardly blame Anna Walls for staying away from Walter. I suspect he's been abusive to her and to her kids. I hope she can find some way to get out of that marriage. More power to her if she has relatives willing to help."

"The Lieutenant only gave us until Friday to close this case." Jim poured himself a second cup of coffee. "It doesn't look good, does it?"

"No, it doesn't." Mal sat at his desk, blowing over the coffee in his mug to cool it. "About our other case. What time is the exhumation scheduled for?"

"Eleven. I know you have an appointment with Titus Powlett at ten. It's gonna take a while to get the casket out of the ground, so don't feel like you have to rush to get to Spring Grove."

"Thanks. I should be there at least by one. I can pick up food for you on my way. Burger and fries?"

"Yeah, that'd be great. Thanks. Peter Reichenbach called late yesterday afternoon to ask when the exhumation would be. I played dumb."

"Good. I wouldn't want him showing up at Spring Grove." Mal leaned forward. "It seems to me something is very wrong there, Jim. Reichenbach's behavior has become erratic. I worry a little about Mary Ellen."

"You know…Peter has said very little about his mother. He's said quite a bit about his father."

"I doubt he remembers much. He was only ten when she died and it was a scary time. Gus was eight, and she doesn't remember a lot about her mother either. She says what she does remember may be more from what her uncle has told her than actual memories."

Mal shuffled through the papers in the Don Martin file, knowing he'd done everything he could, but not wanting to admit failure. Finally, at nine-twenty he left Headquarters to head for Florence.

Who were you, Alice Addleman Reichenbach? This is all I have at this point: a child of the Victorian era. A singer, an unusually pretty girl. Were you reserved? Vivacious? Adventuresome? Did you love both of these young men, the one you married and the one I suspect you had an affair with?

Guinevere popped into his head. An arranged marriage to King Arthur, and then meeting the French knight Lancelot who won her heart. The legends all indicated she loved both men and struggled to remain faithful to Arthur, but eventually gave in to her passion. And Arthur and Lancelot…the knight who swore fealty to his King. The King who returned that love. *But Guinevere didn't die…and Arthur didn't kill Lancelot.*

Titus Powlett was everything Augusta had said, alert, perceptive, intrigued to be interviewed by a detective. "What can I tell you, Detective Mitchell?"

"If you don't object, I'd like to jot down some notes as we talk." Mal pulled a pad from his inside jacket pocket.

"That's fine. Whatever will be helpful." Titus propped his walker next to his chair.

"Peter Reichenbach has told us Wesley Vandergriff and his father were close friends. Did you know Thomas?"

Titus' pale eyes twinkled behind thick glasses. "I certainly did. In fact, I met those men when they were boys…students at Walnut Hills High School. Wesley had just begun to study with me. I was giving organ lessons at Calvary Episcopal Church in Clifton, and Thomas would sometimes come to the church to wait for Wesley to finish his lesson. They were quite a pair. Tom was quieter, but they balanced each other, if you know what I mean. When Wesley started studying with me, he was fourteen. He and Tom were in the same grade."

"Did you see them outside of those lessons?"

"Eventually. I liked Tom. He was a steadfast friend to Wesley, and always encouraged and supported him in whatever he did. When Wes started performing, first on recitals with other of my students, and then giving his first solo recital when he was sixteen, Tom was always on hand. And I sometimes had students come to my place for dessert after a program. Tom was always invited. He may not have been a student, but he was definitely a supporter."

"Wesley lived with his family?"

"His grandmother. Both his parents were deceased. They died when he was young, I believe during a cholera outbreak. They were living in Indiana at the time, and Wesley's grandmother went to Aurora to bring him to Cincinnati. Tom's family treated Wes like another son. He spent a lot of time with them."

Mal jotted notes on his pad. "Interesting. We never think about cholera these days. How different life was then."

"So, you can see how it was that the boys were so close. After they finished high school, Wes stayed here and went to the Conservatory, and Tom headed for Baltimore to study to be a doctor at Johns Hopkins. But Tom was home during the summers. And Wes visited him in Baltimore a few times."

"Did you know Tom's wife, Alice?"

"Oh, yes. Alice and Thomas were neighbors, both lived in big homes in Clifton. They had kind of grown up together, only she was two years younger, and the prettiest child I think I've ever seen. Of course, Wes and Tom thought so, too."

Now we're getting somewhere. "They both took a shine to her."

"Well, Alice started coming around when she was thirteen. At first, they were a happy threesome. Kind of like the Three Musketeers. But as the years passed and she began to grow from being a pretty child to becoming a beautiful young woman, it was apparent they were both vying for her attention."

"But she preferred Tom."

"Not necessarily. Alice's father preferred Tom." Titus shifted in his chair, placing his hands on the arms. "I told you they were neighbors. Both families always assumed they would marry. They were Cincinnati old money, as were all the Clifton gentry. Wesley's grandmother lived in Over-the-Rhine. Working class. You know how this town is. Alice would be expected to marry the doctor from 'aristocracy' rather than the musician, who might be poor all his life." He shook his head. "It's too bad her father didn't recognize Wesley's potential, that he might well become an internationally renowned classical organist."

"Are you saying Alice loved Wesley more but still married Thomas?"

"I believe that's entirely possible. Alice's father, Alphonse Addleman, was a powerful figure in her life, and remember, this was the Victorian era. Unlike your lady, Alice may not have felt free to follow her heart." He chuckled. "For as long as I've known her, Augusta has known who she is, and what she wants."

Malcom laughed. "She is certainly independent. I understand what you're saying. She's the product of a different era, though."

"Not so far removed from Alice's. You must know that people see Augusta as a woman ahead of her time."

Interesting observation about Augusta. But let's stay on topic. "What else do you remember about Alice?"

"She was as sweet as she was pretty. Intelligent and sensitive, with a quiet sense of humor and a great laugh. And she was a talented singer. I think she would have loved to have done more with her music, but her father wasn't very encouraging. So Alice married Thomas and settled into being a doctor's wife."

"And Wesley became the family friend. Peter refers to him as 'Uncle Wes.'"

"So it seemed, but I don't think Wesley ever stopped loving Alice. I suppose he was happy to be with her however he could. But there were times...."

Malcolm waited patiently as Titus collected his thoughts.

"The first two years of their marriage, Tom was in school in Baltimore and Alice stayed here and lived with her parents. She continued to study at the Conservatory, so she spent some time with Wesley there. Through the years Alice would sometimes sing at a church where Wesley was playing. And Tom spent long hours at the hospital; he was quite dedicated to his practice and research. There was opportunity. Mind you, I was never sure about this."

Titus suddenly yawned loudly and seemed almost to doze off. He jerked his head up abruptly. "Then there was this…Wesley came to see me when he learned Alice had died. I've never seen a man so grief-stricken."

"Did he say anything? I mean, specifically?"

"Yes. He said, 'Now there will never be any chance for us.'"

"He hoped Alice would leave Thomas for him," Mal said.

"That's the way I understood it." Another yawn, so prolonged Titus' eyes watered.

"I think I've overstayed my welcome, Mr. Powlett." Mal rose from his chair. "You've been extremely helpful. Thank you so much for speaking with me."

***

Augusta tried to read Malcolm's expression when he came through the door of the nursing home to find her standing next to her car. He stopped and stared at her, dumbfounded.

"I brought lunch," she called out cheerfully.

He strode to her, still staring.

"Well, you have to eat. I brought sandwiches and coffee."

"It's hardly picnic weather, Augusta."

"We can eat in my car. And you can fill me in between bites."

"Mrs. Mitchell, if you don't just beat all." He gave in, chuckling. "What about your lessons?"

"I finished before eleven and canceled my afternoon class."

She saw the frown and added hastily, "My students are ahead of the lesson plans in that class, and anyway, they're all geniuses. And Fritz is in Henrietta Bluefield's tender care. I do have makeup lessons later at the Conservatory. Otherwise, I'm free."

Mal opened the passenger side door and slid in. "Free to see what other mischief you can get into, no doubt."

"I've been good. I honestly gave some thought to just walking in on your interview, but I decided that was a very bad idea." Augusta sat in the back seat of the car and opened a wicker basket, removing napkins, wrapped sandwiches, a bag of chips, a thermos and two plastic mugs.

"You did all this?"

"The nuns in the dining hall did it for me. They love me."

She settled comfortably in the back seat, shaking a napkin across her lap and unwrapping a sandwich. "Chicken salad. The others are sliced roast beef. Oh, and there are cupcakes for dessert."

He continued to stare at her.

"Well…please say something. Yell if you must." She handed him a sandwich.

"I'm trying to figure out what I could yell at you about. There really doesn't seem to be any reason to." He grinned. "This reminds me of the first time we met at Cliffside and you showed up outside the greenhouse after I'd thrown you off the campus."

"Oh, good. I can still surprise you." Augusta opened the thermos and poured him a mug of coffee. She listened quietly, not interrupting as Malcolm repeated his conversation with Titus Powlett.

When he finished, she was thoughtful for a time. "What Titus said about Alice maybe following her heart for the first time in her life. Mal, it sounds as if Alice never thought for herself. Her father made all her decisions. All her choices. I can't imagine living that way."

"No, I'm sure you can't. Titus does seem to believe Wesley and Alice were intimate after her marriage. Poor Wesley. His life was full of promise in so many ways, and yet nothing came to full realization. It seems entirely possible there was an affair and Thomas found out about it, maybe after Alice died. But how? Did Wesley feel so guilty he thought he should confess?"

"Or did Alice tell him before she died? That seems more likely."

"I saw a portrait of her at Peter's yesterday. She truly was a beautiful woman. Fair hair and big dark eyes, and such an appealing face."

"Just as she appeared in the photo I found. You know, I remember meeting Dr. Thomas Reichenbach at a fundraiser several years ago. A benefit for the CPD Police Academy. We actually sat near each other at dinner. He was very pleasant but quiet. I recall thinking his name suited him well. An attractive man, blue eyes, and at that point white hair."

"So, I take it you thought he had what we consider a typical German appearance? Fair hair, blue eyes?"

"Yes, I guess I did. I don't think of Peter that way. Did you ask Titus anything about Peter? If he ever met him as a child?"

"I was going to, but he almost conked out sitting in the chair."

Augusta felt her eyes widen. "Conked out?"

"I mean he was about to fall asleep. It's hard to remember he's over ninety. You were right about how sharp he is." He eyed the half sandwich that remained of their picnic. "Are you going to eat that?"

"It's all yours." She sipped her coffee and unwrapped a cupcake, setting aside the other one for him. "You know…about the way Peter's been acting lately. Is it possible he remembered something? Something he saw or overheard as a child? People can do that. 'Repressed memories' is what I believe they're called. An event triggers them and they can be traumatic."

"Yes, I've heard that."

Augusta handed the cupcake to Mal, aware of his steady blue gaze.

"What?"

"When I was driving over here, I thought about the King Arthur legend. Guinevere being in love with two men at the same time—Arthur and Lancelot. Married to one, unable to resist her attraction to the other. I had thought about it as betrayal, but then Titus made the remark about Alice following her heart."

"You're full of surprises, Detective, to make that connection and then to sympathize with Alice. Can a woman love two men at once? I can't answer that. I only love one."

"I don't know that I've ever said this to you. But you should know how much it means to me that your love is a constant in my life."

Her eyes stung with tears and she inhaled sharply. *What a remarkable thing for him to say.* To her profound annoyance, the tears escaped. Augusta considered it a bane of her existence that she cried so easily.

Malcolm tenderly brushed the tears away. "Sorry, Gus. I didn't intend to make your tear ducts leak."

He pressed her hand after taking the cupcake, continuing to gaze into her eyes.

"I guess I should bring you lunch more often," she finally said.

Malcolm threw his head back and laughed heartily.

Chapter 19
Arthur and Lancelot

It's not even one. I don't have students until three. Augusta left the parking lot, heading for the John Roebling Suspension Bridge which would take her into downtown Cincinnati.

I should head for the Conservatory. I can use this time to select music for some of my students for next semester. She switched on her radio to WGUC, Cincinnati's recently established all-classical radio station.

"...it's generally agreed that the Tristan and Isolde legend pre-dated and influenced the legends of Arthur, Guinevere, and Lancelot, though the stories are similar..." Augusta did a double take. *Guinevere again? Really?* "...a performance arranged for orchestra of probably the best-known music from Wagner's opera, the 'Liebestod' which concludes the work."

While Augusta didn't consider herself an avid fan of Richard Wagner's operas, she loved some of their more brilliant sections of music, and this one from *Tristan und Isolde* she found breathtakingly beautiful. Rather than attempting to drive and listen, she found a turnoff, put her head back and let Wagner's emotional music of love and death wash over her, thinking about Thomas, Alice, and Wesley. Or Arthur, Guinevere, and Lancelot—or King Mark, Isolde, and Tristan.

The music began quietly, with themes which spoke of longing and passion. Wagner wove a sense of doom into the music, and he masterfully used different combinations of instruments as the music continued to build and build to an almost unbearably heart- wrenching climax.

What a tragedy they lived. Thomas, who loved Alice and most likely gave her everything she could want. Alice, who tried to love two men and ended up betraying them both. Wesley, the most tragic figure of all, denied all the promise of his young life.

Wagner's music drew to a quiet conclusion and Augusta wiped her eyes. *We have a good idea of what happened. We may never know exactly how, but it's becoming more apparent why.*

She and Mal would need to discuss Peter further. At this point, he was most important. What would happen to him if he realized he might be Wesley Vandergriff's son?

Arriving at the Conservatory, Augusta spotted Milly chatting with the dean near the reception desk and waved to her. Milly finished her conversation with Dale Williamson and bustled toward Augusta.

"I'm surprised to see you. You're not here on Wednesdays."

"Not as a rule, no. I'm at Cliffside. I rearranged my schedule a bit today." The women continued down the hall to Augusta's studio.

"How was your weekend away?" Milly dropped into a chair across from Augusta's desk.

"Pretty much perfect. You know how beautiful the Poconos are…and what a delightful guy my Uncle Lenny is."

"Yes, I certainly do. Do you remember the first time I met him? He came to Cincinnati to visit you when we were freshmen. I thought he was the most fascinating 'older man' I'd ever met. I guess he was all of thirty."

"He calls you one of his favorite people. He's coming for Christmas."

"Really?" Milly beamed. "Won't that be fun? He's never met Garrett. That should be interesting."

"Millicent—what are you thinking?" Augusta lifted an eyebrow.

"Never you mind. Just planning a little fun."

"At whose expense? Why don't you just tell Garrett 'yes' one of these days? I know he proposes almost daily."

"If you recall, I tried marriage once. I'm very bad at it."

"You haven't tried it with Garrett. Just promise me you'll behave yourself while Len is here."

"I'm not promising anything," Milly chuckled. "Anyway, back to your weekend trip. Did you take Mal to see the Gap?"

"That's the first place we went. We crossed the Delaware at Columbia, drove through Portland, and up Route 611. That's the absolute best way to see the Gap for the first time."

"I'm jealous. It makes me want to go back."

"There's nothing stopping you." Augusta pulled a legal pad from her desk drawer and wrote a name at the top. "Only make it longer than a weekend, it was way too short."

Milly craned her neck to read what Augusta had written. "Selecting music for next semester? Who is that? Oh, Fernando."

"Yes. I'm thinking about the Vaughan Williams *Songs of Travel.*"

"He's done some of those, I'm sure. Maybe 'The Vagabond' and 'Whither Must I Wander'?"

Augusta nodded. "Yes, those two. Some of the best ones he needs to learn."

Milly sat back in her chair. "Meanwhile, back in the past here in Cincinnati…" she prompted.

"Why do you do this to me? You know it's an ongoing investigation and I can't say anything much. An unusual one, though, to be sure." Augusta made a note on her pad.

"'The Roadside Fire,'" Milly read it upside down. "My favorite. Anyway, let's suppose Thomas Reichenbach was involved in a murder back in 1918. Since he can't have been the victim because he died fairly recently, it's possible he killed someone and buried the bones. Obviously, he can't be prosecuted, even if there is strong circumstantial evidence. What happens then?"

"I honestly have no idea. Malcolm has opened a case file." Augusta put down the pad and pen.

"Don't stop what you're doing on my account."

"You're sending mixed signals," Augusta laughed. "Go ahead and talk, I'll listen."

"So, it's an open homicide investigation and hopefully will somehow be closed. Unlike the file on that poor young law enforcement officer, Donald Martin."

"How did you know…oh, right. Garrett. Knows all, sees all, and usually tells you."

Milly leaned forward. "And I've been thinking about your visit to Titus Powlett. What would have prompted you to go and visit him? I love Titus. He's one of the grand old Cincinnati musicians of my time, and I remember more than once hearing him wax eloquent about his student Wesley Vandergriff. Who, as it happened, died in 1918, ostensibly of the Spanish flu. Could your visit to Titus have possibly been to find something out about Vandergriff? Maybe he did not die of influenza?"

"No comment. Anyway, how would Titus know that? You heard Garrett. He told us there was tremendous turmoil during that period. And Vandergriff is buried in Spring Grove Cemetery." *Well, probably not, but I can't tell Milly that.*

"If you say so. Sooner or later Garrett will find out and tell me. But you heard how eloquently he spoke of

Dr. Reichenbach. He's not about to make any of this public knowledge if it can be avoided. What's the point?"

Milly slapped her palms against her knees and stood. "I have to take off. It's time for my next student. This one will be fun. A new student, Jolie Parrish. Remarkable talent for a freshman."

"All these young musicians with such promise," Augusta mused. "Some of them may actually make a career in music. I think Nando has a real chance at being a professional singer."

"It looks that way. So long as the world stays on its axis. The same was thought for Wesley Vandergriff, and we know how that turned out."

***

As always, Malcolm was struck by the beauty and peace of Cincinnati's Spring Grove Cemetery and Arboretum, considered a show place of his city due to its spacious, carefully cultivated grounds, small lakes and ponds, memorial sculptures and chapels. He checked his notepad for directions to Wesley Vandergriff's burial place, but as he drove deeper up into the cemetery, he could see the backhoe that had been at work and found his way to the gravesite. A number of workers were involved in lifting the casket from the vault. Gary was on hand, supervising, and the work was being done quietly and with respect.

Exiting his car, Malcolm noticed the tall, white marble monument that had been temporarily removed from the grave, engraved with Wesley's name, dates of birth and death, and the words, "Well Done, Thou Good and Faithful Servant." At first, he was taken aback that Thomas Reichenbach would have gone to that expense, but remembered he had been told it was provided by a group of church musicians, mostly organists.

If this isn't Wesley, what do we do with that? Maybe bury his bones in this gravesite. He deserves to lie here. he thought it made sense that this should be Wesley's final resting place, receiving the recognition his friends had wanted him to have. Mal cleared his throat hard and ran a hand over his face, a little surprised at how emotional he had suddenly become.

Jim leaned against his car and lifted a hand as Malcolm walked toward him. "No problem getting to the vault, but now they're down putting chains around the casket. It's pretty rusted. This may take a little time."

Mal handed Jim the bag from Frisch's Big Boy as they moved a distance away from the grave to sit on a nearby wrought iron park bench.

"Hey, a Brawny Lad." Jim grinned. "Thanks for remembering."

"Yeah, and onion rings instead of fries. That was your meal the last time we stopped there."

"I'm touched that you remembered, partner," Jim laughed, taking a big bite of the steak sandwich. "What'd you find out from Powlett?"

"I believe we have the motive. It seems Mrs. Reichenbach may not have been as virtuous as her obituary indicated."

"No kidding. Wow. You think Thomas found out and did away with Vandergriff? Maybe a deathbed confession from Alice?"

"Or maybe Wesley confessed to him after Alice died, out of guilt. I'm thinking a crime of passion makes more sense than Thomas planning a murder."

They were interrupted by a heavy crash as the vault and coffin fell apart and dropped back into the ground, causing them both to jump up and stare. Jim ran toward the site and spoke briefly with Gary.

"Oh, great. Well, this is an old grave. We know it can happen." Jim said, returning to his seat. "So, anything else?"

Malcolm filled him in on the rest of his meeting with Titus Powlett. "Augusta brought me lunch." He lifted a warning hand. "Don't even say it. She didn't come inside. She was waiting for me in the parking lot."

"I'm not going to say a thing." Jim chuckled. "Well, maybe just this—have you considered enrolling her in the Academy?"

"First I want to get her to the shooting range. You should have seen her with that shotgun in the Poconos, picking off clay pigeons." Both men laughed.

Mal grew serious. "One thing she said that we need to consider. Peter's erratic behavior recently. Augusta wonders if he somehow was aware of the affair between his mother and his father's close friend. Maybe a childhood memory he's been repressing, that has surfaced because of all of this."

Jim finished his food and looked for a trash container. "That would explain quite a bit. Poor guy could be on the verge of a nervous breakdown."

Malcolm glanced at his wristwatch. "Let's hope we get the body to the morgue before too much longer. If it is Wesley in that casket, we'll just have to consider the bones that were found behind the house are those of a John Doe. That would help put Peter's mind at ease."

"Yeah, but if it's not Wesley in the casket, then we're fairly sure that's who the bones are. In either event, we have to let Peter know."

***

It took a while, but by just before three the casket had been removed from the ground. It was placed into a waiting ambulance and transported quickly to the morgue. After being moved into a refrigerated room, the body was removed from the casket and placed on an examining table.

Malcolm and Jim stood by as Gary did a cursory exam of what were mostly bones. He finally turned to them.

"Based on anecdotal evidence, I can say this is not the body of Wesley Vandergriff. No indication of Marfan Syndrome. This John Doe is approximately five feet ten inches tall, and has short, stubby fingers. There is also no fracture of the left tibia. Remember, these are preliminary findings and my examination won't be complete for several hours. But I don't believe I will find any reason to change what I just told you."

The drive to the Reichenbachs' was quiet. "This is going to be tough," Malcolm noted.

"I'll tell him. No telling how he'll react."

"Are you sure? I can do it."

"No, I think he'll take it better coming from me," Jim insisted. "I'm kind of more the neutral party here. He connects you to Augusta. I don't believe Peter's feeling any too friendly toward musicians these days."

Mal was silent for a moment. "You could be right."

Mary Ellen answered the door. "Good afternoon, Mrs. Reichenbach, may we please speak with your husband?" Jim asked formally.

She looked from one of them to the other. "He isn't here. He left about a half-hour ago. He said he needed to talk to Augusta and he was headed for the Conservatory."

Chapter 20
Recovered Memories

Augusta walked with Lily Myles to the door, handing her a folded slip of paper. "Here's Dr. Lyons' address. He's in the Carew Tower. Remember, no talking or singing until after you've seen him. Try not to be impatient, bronchitis can hang on for a while."

Lily, who had been in tears, gave her a tremulous smile. "I'll try, Professor McKee." Her hand flew to her mouth and Augusta chuckled. "He's expecting you at four-thirty, so grab a cab and get downtown right away."

Poor kid. She'll be fine, but like most young students, she has to learn taking special care of her voice is part of being a singer.

Augusta cleared her desk, preparing to put on her coat and leave the building, when there was a tap on her door.

"Milly?"

To her surprise, Peter Reichenbach burst into her studio, clutching a small briefcase. "I need to talk to you."

"Of course."

Something is very wrong. Peter looked unkempt; his clothes disheveled. She had always thought of him as a very well-ordered person, but now his hair was uncombed, and when he removed his overcoat, she saw his shirt wasn't buttoned properly. Peter's eyes darted around the room as he repeatedly shoved his glasses up his nose.

Augusta watched as he spotted her key, which she had dropped on her desk as she often did. He moved quickly to the desk and grabbed it up, half-running to the door.

"You don't mind if I lock this, do you?" he said, his voice sounding distant and strange. "I don't want us to be interrupted."

Stay calm, Augusta. Let him talk.

Her hands itched to pick up the phone and call someone, just to alert them to her situation. The fear she experienced was more for Peter than for herself. *He's distraught; he needs professional help.*

"No, that's fine," she told him calmly. "If you're more comfortable."

He continued to grip his briefcase with both hands as he perched gingerly on a chair across from her desk. "I have to talk to you." He said again.

"Tell me what I can do for you, Peter."

He didn't say anything for a moment; the only sound in the room was his heel striking the floor as his right leg bounced up and down, seemingly uncontrollably.

"What is it, Peter?"

"All this. All the things that have happened recently." He sighed heavily, while his leg continued to bounce. "I don't even know who I am anymore."

"What do you want…need…to talk about?"

"My father." A long pause. "My mother."

"What about them? You've told me quite a bit about your father, but I haven't heard much about your mother."

"You know that opera? The one by Gustav Holst."

Augusta watched as Peter's attention darted across the room, only to land squarely back on her. "Why did you decide to perform that?" His question sounded accusatory.

"As a matter of fact, John Edmanston chose it and asked me to direct. It was challenging, and I generally like challenges."

"The costumes. The costume for the…for Savitri."

"Yes, the robe she wore." *Where is this headed?* "What about it?"

"Why did you choose that color?"

"No special reason. If you remember, the backdrop—the scrim—resembled a Monet painting. He often used that particular shade of pink, so I decided to have Savitri in a rose-colored robe." *Where in the world is he going with this?*

"You know, I barely remember my mother. Just a few random flashes here and there. She was…" he paused. "I was ten when she died."

"Yes, I recall your telling me that. Remember? When we had lunch recently."

"We had lunch?"

"Two weeks ago." *Doesn't he remember? Tread carefully, Augusta.*

Peter's eyes darted around the room again, this time in quick jerky movements. "My father was a great father."

"Yes, you told me that as well."

Peter lifted the briefcase and laid it across his lap. *Now what?*

"You know what he did?" he asked her, popping the latch. The sudden sound caused her to stiffen her back and catch a breath. "He taught me how to make a blade really sharp. Even with my Boy Scout knife."

He pulled a Scout knife from the case and snapped it open, running his thumb gingerly along the razor-sharp edge.

Dear Lord. Is he threatening me? But why?

"That's…quite impressive. What a nice knife. Did he give it to you?"

Peter set the briefcase down next to his feet and stared at her. "What?"

"Did your father give you that knife."

He stared at the knife as if he'd forgotten it was in his hand.

"Oh…yes, he did. Anyway…that robe…the one Savitri wore. The color. It reminded me of something."

His expression changed, making him appear almost childlike.

"Would you like to tell me about that?" *What am I doing? I'm no psychologist.*

"My mother owned a robe that same color. In fact, it looked a lot like the robe I saw on stage."

A repressed memory that has become a living nightmare for this poor man. Keep him talking. "So, the robe's color reminded you of one you saw your mother in."

"Yes. But there was more. She was singing."

"Your mother?"

"*No.*" He raised his voice in exasperation. "The woman in the opera. She kind of looked like my mother, you know."

Augusta watched in horrified fascination as Peter carelessly tossed the open knife, with its super sharp blade, from one hand to the other.

Did he sharpen it before he came here?

"Isn't that interesting, that Ginny looked like your mother. I wouldn't have known that."

"She sang something to that other character…Death, wasn't it?"

"Yes. The singer represented Death."

"She sang…something like…'you make me real. You give me life…and joy beyond everything else.' I think that's what she sang."

"Yes, that's almost exactly what she sang. How amazing that you remember it so well."

Peter beamed at her, like a child who has been praised for an accomplishment.

Maybe this is what I need to do. He's ten years old again. Maybe even younger. I'm the adult and he wants me to tell him he's being good.

"Peter, how old were you when you heard your mother say that?"

He began to rock back and forth, returning to the time of his memory. "I was five years old. It was very late at night. I heard her in the hallway. I was sick. I had a fever, and I went to find her."

"And she was there with your father."

"*NO!*" He screamed.

He leapt to his feet, gripping the knife and pointing it directly at her, inches from her throat. *Don't stare at the knife, Augusta. Keep looking into his face.*

Her heart pounding. *Stay calm. It isn't me he's angry with; he doesn't know what he's doing.*

"It was all wrong. *Wrong.* My father was away. They were kissing…."

Peter leaned against the desk, lowering the knife but still clutching it. He bit his lip so hard he drew blood. Tears coursed down his face.

"My Uncle Wesley was there," he sobbed. "My mother took me back to my room, and she told me I was dreaming. The fever was making me have a bad dream. So I forgot about it…for a long time."

Augusta kept an eye on the knife, wondering if she could somehow persuade him to put it down on her desk. "And you just remembered this recently," she said.

"It's all these things…you know…the body…and it might be Wesley…and all of this…and the letters said…my father is…isn't my father…what my mother did…" he waved the knife wildly over his head.

Augusta drew in a breath. *Where are the police when you need them most?*

The doorknob rattled, and Mal's voice: "Augusta? Are you all right?"

Thank God thank God thank God. Augusta allowed herself to exhale slightly.

Peter clutched the knife more firmly, again brandishing it in her direction as he glared at the door. "I don't want him in here," he hissed. "Tell him to go away."

"Mal, Peter's here talking with me." Augusta chose her words carefully, fighting to keep her voice from shaking. She prayed Mal would pick up on her hints. "We're having a nice talk about his mother, and how his father taught him to sharpen his knife, but he'd prefer you wait outside."

"I'm not sure I can do that. Peter, may I come in, please?"

"*NO.* I'm talking to Augusta," he yelled. He spun around to face the door.

"Mal, I think Peter has a little more to tell me. Something he remembered that happened long ago. It's fine."

Peter turned back to face Augusta. She forced herself to smile warmly at him as he peered at her suspiciously. "You know, Peter, all of us have been worried about you. We have an idea of how difficult all this has been for you. I think it's been much, much worse than any of us realized."

Peter stared at her again, and blinked hard. "Augusta?"

"Yes, Peter. I'm here and I want to help you. We all want to help you." *Stay with me, Peter. Come back to the present.*

"We?"

"Yes. My husband is here, and he's been just as worried about you as I have. Will you let me unlock the door so he can come in?"

Peter blinked again, glancing about the room, confused. "How long have I been here?"

"Not long."

He stared at the knife and then at her.

"It's all right, Peter. Nothing has happened."

This poor soul. He's just gone through a psychotic break of some kind.

"Did you say Malcolm is here?"

"Yes, he's right outside. But the door is locked. May I unlock it so he can come in?"

Peter squared his shoulders and wiped his face with his sleeve, still gripping his knife.

"Why not put the knife down?" Augusta implored. "I don't think you need it now."

"Yes…all right." He slowly laid it on her desk and sank back into his chair. Augusta felt an enormous knot in her stomach untie itself.

"May I have my key?" She pointed to the floor where the key had fallen.

"Oh. Here." Peter reached down, picked it up and extended it toward her.

"Thank you." Her hand trembling slightly, Augusta quickly went to the door. When she opened it Mal nearly fell into the room. She was sure he had been standing with his ear pressed against the door. She felt his strong hand on her back and almost wept with relief.

"Peter isn't feeling well," she said, managing to sound calm. "He needs help."

She watched Mal assess the situation in seconds: the knife on her desk, Peter in his chair with shoulders slumped forward, signaling defeat, the open briefcase leaning against his chair.

What else is in there? She wondered.

Lifting an eyebrow at Malcolm, Augusta returned to her desk. "Peter, did you have something else you wanted to show me?"

Malcolm stood quietly to the side as Augusta saw Jim Edmonds ease into the room, pressed against the wall.

"There are letters." Peter stared hard at Malcolm, then at Augusta. "Letters for Malcolm to read. I just read them last night."

He sighed again, dropping his head into his hands. "I'm so tired." He looked up at Malcolm. "I'd like to go home now."

Mal laid a hand on Peter's shoulder. "What about this, Peter." He leaned down, speaking quietly. "Detective Edmonds—Jim—is here, too. He can drive you home in his car, and Augusta and I will be there in a few minutes."

241

Augusta held her breath when Peter, startled, turned to see Jim, but the seasoned detective assumed a casual calm and Peter relaxed.

"Yes, okay. We can do that." Peter suddenly reached for the knife, sending both men on high alert, but he closed it and replaced it in the briefcase. "I'll give you the letters when you come to my house. I can explain how I got them."

Jim helped him stand. "Why don't I carry that for you?" He motioned to the briefcase.

"This? Yes. Okay. That's fine." He turned toward the door, but stopped. "Oh. Malcolm and Jim? The letters will answer all your questions."

"Ready?" Jim tucked an arm under Peter's elbow and led him slowly from the room.

Once they were out of earshot, Augusta ran into Malcolm's arms, choking back sobs.

"Let it out, Gus." His voice shook. "I was scared, too."

They held each other for long moments, clinging gratefully to each other, fully aware the outcome could have been entirely different.

Chapter 21
Secrets

Limp with relief that she wasn't hurt, Mal held Augusta close and let her cry.

"Are you sure you're okay?"

"I will be." She pulled back and gazed at him. "Oh, Mal. That was so sad."

He stared at her. "*Sad?*" He spat out through gritted teeth. "It was terrifying. He could have killed you."

"He didn't menace me. Not really. He wanted to show off the knife. His father showed him how to make it really sharp. You can't charge him with anything."

"Oh, can't I? Just watch. I don't believe for one minute he didn't threaten you with that knife."

"He didn't, Mal. Not intentionally."

"You have to explain that."

"He was holding the knife, and he did point it at me."

"Dear God, Augusta."

"But he didn't even see me," she added hastily. "He was back in the past remembering the fear and confusion he'd felt as a child. I won't press charges. Peter was…traumatized. He was irrational, but I never believed he would hurt me."

"Gus, if he had harmed you and I'd had the opportunity, I might have killed him. You *know* how big a deal that is to me. And now you're telling me you won't prosecute?"

"Please listen. I think you would feel differently—wouldn't be so angry—if it had been someone other than me that you thought was in danger."

"You're damned right I'm angry. And this isn't the first time I've had to face the possibility of losing you." He stared hard at her. "You do realize I haven't *almost lost* Jim as much as I've almost lost you, don't you?"

"Mal." She pressed her hands against his chest, gazing earnestly into his face. "If you had been in the room with him, you would see it differently."

"The hell I would."

"He was a child. A five-year-old child who saw and heard something he never should have witnessed. His mother, having an intimate moment with a man who wasn't his father. And she convinced him to forget it. He was right back in that moment, confused, bewildered, bragging about his father who gave him a Scout knife…remembering his mother as a beautiful woman…"

"That's no excuse," Mal said.

Augusta put a finger to his lips. "He reacted as a child would have, and then he found his way back to

244

reality. He's no danger to me or to anyone. He needs help. He may be in therapy for a long time."

He stared at her. "You're asking me to try to understand rather than judge him?"

"That's one way to put it. Or maybe, 'I find you guilty, but you've already served your sentence.'"

Malcolm allowed himself the ghost of a smile. "More like, 'credit for time served,' but I get your point."

She kissed him and held him close for a moment. "Those letters. Did you hear him say something about not knowing who his real father was? Mal...he knows. Something in those letters gave him the knowledge that Wesley Vandergriff is his biological father. What would that do to any man? Finding out something that earth-shattering."

Malcolm took a deep breath and pulled her closer. "You never cease to amaze me, Mrs. Mitchell. What a thing to have to go through...and I mean you, not Peter Reichenbach." He put his hands on her shoulders as he looked into her face. "You had a crazy person on your hands. You defused what could have been a very dicey situation. And you did it with courage and compassion."

Augusta gazed at him and kissed him softly. He embraced her tightly and she sighed as she rested her head on his shoulder for a moment, then pulled back and glanced at her wristwatch.

"We should go, but first I need to call Henrietta and tell her we'll be late getting home. I asked her to stay until five and it's nearly that now. I can take my car and leave the Reichenbachs' earlier than you do if necessary."

Malcolm put an arm around her waist. "I'm not comfortable with you driving after what just happened. Ask her to stay until eight. We can pick up your car tomorrow."

Augusta leaned against him again. "Thank you. That's a much better plan."

***

Jim met them at the door to the Reichenbach house. "He's getting cleaned up. He's much calmer now, but Mary Ellen wants to call his doctor."

He ran a hand over his crew cut. "Mal, much as I dislike doing it, we have to arrest him. He was holding Augusta hostage. Threatening her with a deadly weapon. Should we take him to the psych ward at General Hospital?"

"We're not arresting him. Gus won't press charges. She says Peter was temporarily insane and he wasn't threatening her."

Jim looked from one of them to the other. "I don't like it."

"I don't like any of it," Malcolm said. "From the moment Fritz dug up that bone. Let's hear what he has to say before we do anything."

Strains of music wafted from the library, but this time the music was peaceful, ethereal. Mal glanced at Augusta, lifting an eyebrow.

"Faure's *Requiem*," she told them. "I've sung the soprano solo a number of times, often at a funeral. The entire piece is as lovely as this section."

246

"Good," Mal said. "A lot different from what he's been listening to when we were here before."

They waited in the library, and soon Mary Ellen and Peter joined them, Peter in a robe, apparently fresh out of the shower, carrying an envelope. He waved them toward seats. "Mary Ellen wants to call my doctor, and it's probably a good idea. Augusta, I am so sorry about what I did. I'm not even sure what happened."

"I understand, Peter. And no harm was done." She glanced in Mal's direction. He set his jaw but didn't comment.

"Before my wife calls my doctor, I need to tell you what I learned last night. I had begged you not to exhume the body in Spring Grove, because I feared it wasn't Wesley. What I read last night confirmed my worst fears."

"I have coffee brewing," Mary Ellen said. "I'll bring it in."

Peter sat down, glancing around at them. "My father died five years ago of a heart attack. I hadn't known he was ill; in fact, I don't know that he was aware he had any cardiac problems. After his death I cleaned out his apartment and among his belongings found a box which had some miscellaneous papers in it. I wasn't even sure what they were, but I brought it here to look through them at some point.

"Then Pete Junior was accepted at Juilliard, and we got busy getting him settled in New York. And our daughter Emily was married the following year. I almost forgot about the box. But when I first glanced through it, something struck me. A sealed envelope, which had written across it in red ink the date '1968.' At the time, it struck me as odd, but most of the other items in the box were mundane—meetings from various boards my father served on, receipts for travel, that kind of thing, so I thought it was probably a mistake and he had meant to write '1958' on it. I was very busy getting dad's estate settled and disposing of his furniture and other household items, so you can understand why it went out of my mind. But it popped into my head last night—mainly because of the date. 1968 would be fifty years since my mother's death. Fifty years since the pandemic that turned the world upside down."

He sighed. "Last night, I opened the envelope. It contained four letters. One from my father to me. The other three were love letters. Letters from Wesley Vandergriff to Alice—my mother."

He drew a smaller envelope from the large one, opened it and removed several sheets of paper. "Here's the letter my father wrote me. It's not dated, but I think perhaps he wrote it not long before he died. This is what he wrote...."

Peter, if you should read the enclosed letters—and I haven't yet decided whether I should keep them or dispose of them—I want you to know, first and foremost, that I forgave both of them many years ago. I hope you can as well.

That said, I was never able to forgive myself for what happened, and I don't expect that you will ever forgive me, either. In a moment of uncontrolled rage, I killed Wesley Vandergriff.

I managed to successfully conceal my horrific act by hiding Wesley's body and then falsifying records and having an indigent influenza victim buried in Spring Grove Cemetery in his stead. I told myself it was to protect you. I still believe that was my main motivation for doing so, but I cannot forgive myself for taking a man's life. And not just any man. A man I loved like a brother.

Peter paused in his reading, removing his glasses and wiping his eyes. Mary Ellen returned with a tray and Jim stood and placed it on the coffee table for her. She sat to pour, first taking a cup to her husband, who sipped it gratefully. Except for the lovely music which continued to play, the room was silent.

Peter picked up the letter again, his hand noticeably shaking. "I can't…" his voice choked with emotion. "Mary Ellen, will you finish it, please?"

She moved to sit beside her husband, pressed his shoulder, took the letter and began to read.

When your mother died, I was out of my mind with grief. The medical crisis I had been dealing with for weeks only increased the stress and anguish. As she lay dying, she whispered to me, saying, 'Forgive me, Thomas. There are letters in my bottom dresser drawer, in the back. Please don't judge us too harshly.'

Mal gazed at Augusta. She had been right; a deathbed confession from Alice about her affair with Wesley. Augusta's eyes were swimming with tears.

I couldn't bring myself to look for the letters until two days after Alice's funeral. I think I suspected what I would learn—that the two of them had been lovers, and that Wesley was your biological father. Perhaps you've figured that out already. I was able to confirm it a few years later when blood type tests were developed. My blood type group is O and yours is AB, so no matter what your mother's blood type was, you couldn't be my son.

What they did was wrong. But what came from it was you, a wonderful man I was privileged to spend the remainder of my life with. And for that I shall be eternally grateful—

even to Wesley. While I was not your biological father, I hope I was your father in every other way possible.

Mary Ellen handed the letter to Peter, who had regained his composure. He refolded it as he said, "That's the end of his letter, and it doesn't give particulars as to how and when he took Wesley Vandergriff's life. That will remain a mystery. Or why he had contracted for the patio not long before my mother became ill, but I think I have a possible explanation for that. Dad was friendly with the mason who did the work. He told me at one time Mr. Bright's wife worked at the hospital. Work for everyone was scarce, and my guess is he hired Mr. Bright to build the patio mainly to help out their family." He replaced the letter in the envelope.

"These are for you to use as necessary." Peter sighed as he handed the envelope to Malcolm. "I would like to have them back at some point. I still have some hope that it might be possible to allow this family secret to remain just that—a family secret. I can't see what good could possibly come from revealing it after nearly fifty years, when all three people involved are dead." He sighed again, and turned to Mary Ellen.

"I guess you should call Dr. Morton."

Mary Ellen nodded and left the room.

"I suppose I'm to be arrested for what I did to Augusta. Will you need me to make a statement at City Hall?" Peter asked.

Mal leaned forward. "That won't be necessary, Dr. Reichenbach. Augusta has chosen not to press charges."

Peter turned to Jim. "And you agree?"

"I concur with my partner. We will need to turn in a report about this open homicide case, but I see no reason—nor does Mal, I'm sure—that all of this can't be done quietly. The case will be closed because of 'death of the offender.' I believe the only item of any interest to the public is the fact human remains were found in a backyard in Hyde Park."

"Charlie Worthington has addressed that," Augusta said. "His story is they were most likely from an old Indian burial ground and have been shipped off somewhere for further study."

Peter visibly relaxed. "God bless Charles Worthington. Bless all of you for being so understanding."

Mary Ellen returned. "Dr. Morton is on his way. He'll be here in about ten minutes. What should we tell him?"

Malcolm stood. "We're all leaving, Mrs. Reichenbach. What happens between your husband and his medical team is considered privileged information, as I'm sure you know."

He lifted the envelope. "I would like to read through these. It may help when we attempt to reconstruct the events of the case. I should be able to get them back to you quickly. May I have your permission to make copies?"

Peter pushed himself a little unsteadily to his feet, and Mary Ellen rushed to his side to support him. "By all means. I may request that Dr. Morton see about admitting me to General Hospital for a time. I'm sure he can find a reason. Exhaustion, maybe? Hopefully, he won't put me in the psych ward. But there's a clinic near Dayton which might be helpful. I know I need professional therapy."

As they were on their way out, Mal spoke quietly to Mary Ellen. "Here's my card. It has my home phone written on the back. If you need anything at all please call. And please, let us know how Peter is."

She nodded gratefully. "Thank you. I will."

Malcolm, Augusta, and Jim left the house, each lost in their own thoughts.

"We'll run you home first," Mal told Jim when they reached the car. "Then I need to get Augusta home. We'll pick up her car tomorrow."

"It's been some day," Jim commented. "You okay, Augusta?"

"I will be. Right now, I want to go home and hug Fritz."

"I get that," Jim said. "I plan to spend the rest of the evening with my kids, too."

After sharing a smile, the three sat in silence the rest of the drive home.

Chapter 22
Star-Crossed Lovers

7:00 p.m.

They heard Fritz barking as soon as they left the car. Augusta ran into the house and dropped to her knees, burying her face against the dog's neck as he whined and wagged all over.

"You're home earlier than you thought," Henrietta Bluefield commented. "Fritzer and I just came in from a nice long walk, and he's been fed. He should be fine for the night."

"Thank you for staying late, Mrs. Bluefield." Malcolm patted the pup's head. "It was a big help."

"Oh, no trouble at all, Detective."

He helped her on with her coat as she added, "Mrs. Worthington dropped by earlier with a casserole she said was a thank you for your recent hospitality. It's in the fridge and it looks delicious. Chicken Divan, and she even brought rice."

"Perfect." Augusta stood, continuing to pet her dog. "I was just trying to think what to fix. Peggy's timing is impeccable."

"Well, I'll see you on Friday. Good night. Bye, Fritzer."

Augusta stepped out of her stilettos, carefully placing them out of the dog's reach. Mal went into the kitchen and removed the casserole from the refrigerator, peeking under the foil wrapping. "This looks great. Peggy's a terrific cook."

They soon sat down to eat and Malcolm rested the envelope Peter had given him on the table. "I know you're as curious as I am to read Wesley's letters."

"Peter said there were three. How do you want to do this? Shall we take turns reading them aloud?"

"I'd prefer that. Why don't you read two and I'll read one? You're the performer." He opened them and spread them carefully on the table, aware of the age of the paper. "They're all dated. 1907, 1908, and 1913."

"Let's read them in order." Augusta took a drink of water as Mal handed her the first letter. The somewhat faded, flowery script seemed to echo who Wesley had been, the exuberant, brilliant young musician.

My beloved,

No words will ever express the joy I knew last night in your embrace. At long last, my Alice allowed herself to be the passionate, exciting woman I have always known her to be. To live the kind of love I've heard her sing about, as we became lovers through our shared passion for music.

I know, out of our love for Thomas, we can never be together again as we were last night. But knowing you just that once will last me a lifetime. I'll make it last a lifetime. I know there is no way you could leave Thomas and run away with me...even to Europe. That is a dream that will remain a dream. You made a choice that I completely understand, a choice for a good life with a good man who will provide for you and your children as I might never be able to.

My prayer is that you will begin to sing again. I mean sing as I know you can. Even though pursuing a career in opera is not in your future, give yourself the joy of singing the music you love best. I know you can find a way, even though I must not be a part of it.

My beloved angel, if ever you need me, I am here for you. I agree that Thomas must *never know about last night. I will think of you, love you, and cherish you every moment of my life. Never forget that.*

I was in paradise for a time last night. I knew ecstasy.

Your adoring
Wesley

Augusta touched the letter almost reverently. "Mal—Alice was a singer. Oh, I know people have mentioned that, but it appears she had a real gift. Or at least, Wesley thought she did, and I doubt he would have said so if there weren't at least some truth in it."

"Written after the first time they made love, obviously without planning to. And they agreed it couldn't happen again."

As they continued to talk, they gathered up the items on the table and went together to the kitchen to scrape plates and wash and put away dishes and cutlery.

"We've been talking about the Arthurian triangle but this first letter makes me believe we've been wrong about that," Augusta said. "They were drawn together by their passion for music. He played for her. That can be a strong bond, particularly if both share the emotion in the music."

Mal pulled a beer from the refrigerator as Augusta poured herself a glass of pinot grigio before they returned to the alcove.

"You mean like you and Jean-Luc?" He gave her a wry grin, referring to a romance from Augusta's past when she lived and studied in Paris after she finished college.

Augusta punched his arm. "I've told you, I wasn't in love with Jean-Luc. Well, not really. But yes, we became close because of exactly that—spending time together exploring emotional, passionate music. A lot of musicians marry for that very reason. The marriages don't always last, but it's how the romance begins."

She took a sip of wine. "Having a career as an opera singer was daunting for women in the Victorian era. I know this was slightly past that, but I think Alphonse Addleman would never have allowed his daughter to attempt it. It would have been beneath his dignity. It took an extremely strong woman to make a career during that time."

Mal thoughtfully sipped his beer. "I'm thinking Alice should have married Wesley. Being a dutiful daughter, she turned him down and accepted the doctor. And perhaps regretted it. Wonder what happened that finally ignited their romance?"

"Read the next one."

Mal cleared his throat and moved the second letter closer. "It's dated 1908."

My only love,

I am to be a father. I keep repeating the words to myself and I cannot stop smiling.

It amazes me how sure you are that the child you carry is mine and not Thomas', but you assure me you know. That one night, after all the months we had been apart, has resulted in a new life being created. You say you know it was meant to be, which makes me fairly weep with joy. That night you came to me with such a need to be comforted. Another night in paradise, but that must be the last.

I want to be a part of this miraculous child's life as much as I can, though I know my parentage can never be revealed. To the world, this will be Thomas' child. It must be our secret. But such a joyful secret.

Please cherish yourself, my dearest. I cannot begin to express the happiness you have given me.

Your adoring
Wesley

Mal gazed at Augusta. "It seems they stayed apart for a long time. Over a year. Then something happened...wouldn't you love to know what he was referring to about her needing to be comforted? And they gave in to their feelings for each other again."

"This is such a sad story. Poor Alice. Poor Wesley."

"Poor *Thomas*. They both betrayed him, even though they cared for him." Mal took a swig of beer. "How could she have possibly known she conceived Peter during that tryst? I'm sure she was being a proper wife to Thomas. The child would more likely have been his."

"Considering the times, and who Alice was, I don't think she'd seen a gynecologist, so she was pretty much an innocent. But I've had married friends tell me they knew exactly when they had conceived a child. Maybe Thomas was away for a fairly long time. We know those first two years of their marriage, he was in school in Baltimore and she was living with her parents. Maybe he had to go back for some reason, to finish a course or something. Obviously. Thomas never suspected."

Mal glanced through the letter again. "Well, this time they don't seem to think they might never be lovers again. It's implied, but it's more a sense they'll have to be careful."

He slid the third letter closer to her. "This was 1913—when Peter was five. That would have been the year he had that experience of seeing them together."

Augusta glanced at the brief letter. "This one addresses exactly that event."

My dearest,

After last night, we have no choice but to end our physical relationship once and for all. It frightens me to think how Peter may have been affected by seeing us together. We simply cannot take the chance of that happening ever again. I will not come to the house when Thomas is away, only when he is home. And you must never come to my apartment. Henceforth we can see each other only as fellow musicians.

That will have to be enough to satisfy our souls, sharing the music that gives us both such joy. It grieves me to think how deeply we have wronged Thomas. The possibility he could learn of our betrayal through our son is unthinkable.

Maybe when years pass and Peter is older, we can reconsider. But we cannot think of that now. First and foremost, we must think of our remarkable son whom we love so dearly, his well-being and happiness.

Farewell for now, my angel. I will cherish the memory of every moment we have been together.

Your adoring
Wesley

Mal pulled the letter closer and quickly reread it. "That seems to have been a firm decision. And it does seem they were together only a few times during that six-year period—1907 until 1913."

"Well, as beautiful as the letters are, and as much as I love feeling I know Alice and Wesley better, I don't know that they are helpful so far as trying to come up with how the murder was committed."

"I'm not so sure. For one thing: imagine reading these words two days after you've buried your beloved wife. Learning that she and your closest friend had an affair over a period of years. That she believed the child Thomas shared with her was not his, but Wesley's. Stressed beyond belief trying to care for people with a disease that is totally out of control, and after losing your wife to that same disease."

"Yes, I hear what you're saying. An attorney would say 'goes to state of mind,' correct?" She leaned her head on a hand, elbow propped on the table. "Thomas was out of his mind. Are you thinking Wesley, equally bereft, came to the house to offer his condolences? Because of the pandemic I doubt he would have been allowed to attend the funeral."

"That could be what happened. I don't know that Thomas intended to kill him. Maybe knowing what he'd learned, and then seeing Wesley caused him to snap. But…." he paused. "The knife. It was probably late at night. Wesley would have known Thomas wouldn't be home during the day because he was back at work. There would have been no reason for the men to go outside. The Worthington's kitchen is just off the patio, isn't it?"

"Yes, it is. Say for some reason they were in the kitchen. Didn't Herbert Bright say something about Thomas leaving for the hospital as soon as they started to put down the flagstone? He was back on duty, working long hours. He may have been in the kitchen eating when Wesley showed up."

"Sounds entirely plausible. And we know from Peter his father liked to keep sharp knives around. So, there they are in the kitchen, and Thomas has a sharp knife at his disposal."

Augusta sat up straight. "I believe Wesley had no intention of saying anything about what had happened between him and Alice. It's apparent from his letters. They hoped Thomas would never learn of it."

"I agree. But when Wesley started to offer his condolences, and Thomas knew about the deception…he tells us how he reacted." Malcolm unfolded Thomas' letter.

"'In a moment of uncontrolled rage, I killed Wesley Vandergriff.' Stabbed him viciously in the throat. When he regained control of himself and faced what he had done, he realized he had to dispose of Wesley's body. He had the perfect opportunity to get it out of sight forever. Bury it in the backyard, then get the masons to come back early the next day and complete the patio. No one would ever know."

"When do you think he decided to find a John Doe to bury in Spring Grove?"

"Oh, fairly quickly, I would guess. Maybe later that same day. He knew Wesley had many friends who would start to ask questions within a few days."

"Thomas Reichenbach almost committed the perfect crime. Well, in a way, he did. And then he spent decades trying to live with himself."

Augusta paused for a long moment, then rested a hand on Malcolm's arm. "Mal…if Thomas were alive today, even if he didn't confess…"

"Don't go there, Augusta." Malcolm said in a tone that brooked no argument. "You know the answer. He murdered a man."

She sighed. "I know. I'm grateful Peter will be spared that."

"Remember what the ghost of Hamlet's father told him about the queen? 'Leave her to heaven,' even though she was complicit in his father's murder. Thomas' judgement is for a higher power to determine."

Augusta leaned close to him and caressed his face, gazing into his eyes. "My strong, tough detective, who loves opera and can quote Shakespeare."

"Only *Hamlet*." He stood. "I'm getting another beer. Would you like more wine?"

She nodded and he returned from the kitchen with the pinot grigio, moving his chair so he could sit beside her. "That thing you were talking about. Sharing emotional, passionate music with another musician and one thing leading to another." He gave her a lopsided grin. "Are you ever sorry you didn't marry a musician but ended up with a cop?"

"If I'd married young, I would have married a musician. But that wasn't to be. And until you came along and swept me off my feet—" she smiled at his expression—"I hadn't met anyone I wanted to spend my life with."

"I'm not sure who swept who off whose feet," Malcolm chuckled. "The thing is, in a way, I can understand the connection Wesley and Alice felt because of music." He gazed into Augusta's eyes. "Do you remember the first time you sang to me? I mean, really sang directly to me, while I was sitting next to you on the piano bench? It wasn't long after our first night together. You sang a couple of love songs. I think in French. I'm not sure you realized how—well, how magical that was. Sharing your music so intimately."

"I do remember." She ran a hand across his chest. "One song was Duparc's 'Extase.' Probably the most sensual love song ever written."

"I'll agree with that assessment, Professor McKee." He kissed her softly.

"I love that you appreciate the music that is my life." She moved closer to him. "We manage to make our own music, don't we?"

"That we do," he murmured against her neck.

Chapter 23
Two Cases Put to Rest

Thursday, November 11
4:00 p.m.

Malcolm slowly reviewed every piece of paper in the Donald Martin file, stopping when he came to the funeral notice that had appeared in *The Cincinnati Morning Call*.

MARTIN
Donald, beloved husband of Gail Langley Martin, son of Claude and Allie Martin, Brother of Mrs. Christine McCauliffe, Mrs. Lelia Fields, Mrs. Ruth Blankenship, Mrs. Georgia Carpenter, Earnest, Earl and Ray Martin; Saturday, March 11, 1961. Friends may call at the W. Mack Johnson Funeral Home, 1309 E. McMillan St., Walnut Hills, Monday from 4 to 9 P.M. Service at the Concordia Lutheran Church, 1524 Race St., Tuesday, March 14, at 10 A.M. F.O.P. service Monday, 7:30 P.M.

As he read, he mentally filled in some details: *Don was twenty-nine when he was murdered, an exemplary cop who had received several citations while on the force, including one from Chief Schrotel. His wife Gail, secretary to Henry Sandman, was one of us, too. Making it even more of a tragedy.*

He well remembered the Fraternal Order of Police service. Members of the force still in shock, there to honor their fallen brother. A solemn remembrance, followed by a repast in the hall, the exchange of many memories. Not a few tears shed, most unabashedly.

With a sigh, he went to Lieutenant Kramer's office and tapped on the door. His supervisor looked up when he came in. "You might as well take this. I've run into a dead end again. Walter Walls is an animal on the prowl waiting to kill again and I can't prove he did it. I sure hate to see it go cold."

"Well, it may be officially considered cold, but I expect there'll be more attempts to nail Walls. It's hard to believe he won't end up in jail again, which might provide another opportunity."

"Walls is evil, boss. I fully expect him to murder someone else."

Another tap at the door. Jim stuck his head in. "Finished with this report, Lieut. At least we've closed one case this week." He laid the file on Kramer's desk.

"Have you heard anything from Mrs. Reichenbach?" his supervisor asked.

"Not since we left there last night. She was talking about having Dr. Reichenbach admitted to General Hospital, at least for a time," Jim said.

"He's had to deal with a lot." Mal added. "I gave her my card, and I think Augusta planned to see if she could reach her this morning to see if she needed anything."

"Is your wife okay? The three of you had quite a day yesterday."

"She's fine. Augusta is one of the most resilient people I've ever known," Mal told Kramer.

"Both of you, take the day off tomorrow."

"You mean it?" Jim asked, grinning.

"Unless you hear from me otherwise, come back in Monday morning. Things are quiet right now."

"Copy that." Jim smacked his hands together.

"Are you sure?" Mal asked.

"Beat it. We'll give you a call if we need you."

***

Augusta turned into her driveway, pleased to see that Mal was already home. Fritz met her at the door, spinning in circles until she calmed him down.

"I'm glad to see you, too, Fritzy." She patted his flanks and ruffled his head.

"We have enough of Peggy's casserole left to heat up for dinner," Mal called from the kitchen.

"That sounds perfect."

Augusta went into the kitchen and wrapped her arms around him, kissing him.

Malcom pulled back and lifted an eyebrow. "Any special reason for that?"

"I do so love you," she said, kissing him again. "Sorry I'm late. I stopped by to see Mary Ellen

271

Reichenbach. She called me earlier from General Hospital and asked if I would. She wanted to catch me up on Peter. Let me run upstairs and change and I'll help with dinner."

Fritz followed at her heels. She returned quickly in slacks and a sweater, the dog again right behind her. "I'm afraid we've been neglecting you, Fritzy, while we were off solving the case you put in motion."

"What are you talking about?" Mal chuckled. "This dog has three adoring adults spoiling him constantly."

Augusta laughed, washed her hands and removed salad fixings from the refrigerator. "How nice that you're home early."

"Yes, Jim and I completed our paperwork on both cases we've been working on and our boss let us leave. In fact, he gave us the day off tomorrow."

They served their plates and moved into the alcove, where their puppy took up his usual position, watching as they ate.

"Is he always going to do that?" Augusta asked.

"You know he is. You never know when a bite might hit the floor instead of somebody's mouth."

They smiled at each other. "Tell me about the Reichenbachs."

"Peter's been sedated and slept most of the day. Mary Ellen has made arrangements for him to be admitted to the clinic in Kettering Monday. She plans on taking him home on Saturday so he can spend the weekend with her, and then she'll drive him up there. They haven't talked much, but he did ask her to see about two things."

"What were they?"

"He would like to have Wesley buried in the Spring Grove plot. And she said they'd also pay for whatever was necessary for the John Doe to be interred."

Mal nodded. "I thought that would probably be what he'd want to do. What else?"

"He'd like to have Wesley's watch. He remembers Wesley telling him once that it would be his when he was grown up."

"That can be arranged. Since the case is closed, it's no longer evidence."

Augusta took a drink of water. "Mary Ellen told me a little more about Peter's...about Thomas." She paused. "But you know, I believe Peter will always think of Thomas as his father. Anyway...she said after Thomas retired, they spent quite a bit of time together. He liked to come to the house and talk with her."

"You said she's a writer. Fiction or non-fiction?"

"Non-fiction. She's only written a couple of books, and world history is her special interest. She wrote a study of Mahatma Gandhi's years in South Africa."

Mel lifted his eyebrows. "No kidding. That's ambitious. Any special reason?"

"She said she found him a fascinating individual. She'd like to do a second volume about his time in India." Augusta dabbed her mouth with her napkin. "Mary Ellen said seeing *Savitri* last week reminded her of some conversations she had with Thomas. About Hindu philosophy."

"That part about nothing being real except God?"

"He was intrigued with that thought, and the idea of reincarnation. The belief is the soul can return in another body and continue to learn and strive to reach higher levels of spirituality, until they finally attain *nirvana*— only the Hindus call it *moksha*. To be reunited with God. Sometimes on this journey the soul can atone for past transgressions."

"The kind of transgression Thomas committed."

"Yes, I think that's why the idea appealed to him. Although he spent his entire life trying to atone for killing Wesley, don't you think? Doing good at every opportunity that presented itself."

Mal gazed off into the distance. "Despite what I do…I don't believe I will ever truly understand why a human would deliberately murder another."

"Yet you fought in the war."

"War is different. Nations declare war on each other, and it's usually the young men who slaughter each other at the command of their leaders. It's grim, but there are trained armies pitted against each other. Outside of war, killing someone means taking the life of someone you most likely know, or you're making a deliberate choice to kill in the course of committing a crime. Like Walls killing Don Martin."

Augusta sat back and studied Malcolm's face. "This has all been difficult for you, hasn't it?" she said softly. "Revisiting the Donald Martin case. And then stumbling across a complicated case from decades ago."

"Well, they're both pieces of paper in files at this point. The Martin file was officially retired as a cold case today." Malcolm stood and picked up his plate. "I'm going to take Fritz for a walk."

No wonder he's in a mood, Augusta thought as she watched them leave.

She cleaned the kitchen, and when man and dog returned, Malcolm seemed in better spirits.

"He's a good dog. He's responding really well to 'heel.'" He kissed her briefly. "I'm glad we have him."

"I am, too. And he *is* a good boy."

"Let's listen to some music and then turn in, okay? I'm kind of beat."

I don't think it's physical fatigue. You seem weary at heart to me, my love.

"That sounds good," she agreed.

"I'd rather not hear opera tonight. Maybe something like that pretty piece Mary Ellen had on the Reichenbachs' stereo last night. Do you have that one?"

"No, but I have something equally calming." She went to the stereo. "This is called *The Lark Ascending.* One of my favorite pieces by Vaughan Williams."

Mal leaned back, closed his eyes, and Augusta watched as he allowed the soothing, uplifting music to wash over him. The lovely sounds of an English countryside filled the room, the violin the lark, swooping, ascending, descending, one final upward flight with the sense the bird had broken free of earth and disappeared into the heavens.

Malcom opened his eyes, the intense blue of his gaze turning her heart over as it always did.

"That was beautiful. How do you do that, bride? Always know just what I need?"

She moved closer. "What's troubling you, Malcolm? You seem very down."

He kissed her. "I'll be okay. I just need to get a good night's sleep."

***

Augusta woke and reached for Malcolm. Finding he wasn't there she pulled on a robe and quietly went downstairs. She found him sitting in the dark, legs outstretched, arms across the back of the sofa, Fritz curled up at his feet. Augusta eased next to him, pressing her head against his shoulder, resting a hand on his chest. Malcolm turned and looked at her, touching her face gently.

"Do you want to talk?"

"Yeah, I do." He ran a hand through his hair. "I told you I handed in the Martin file today. I never told you this."

Malcolm sighed heavily and paused for a long moment. "The night Martin was killed my former partner and I were on duty. We were the first detectives on scene."

"Oh, Malcolm. How awful that must have been. Why haven't you said anything about it?"

"I've been trying to be objective about the case. We've been working it for four years, but Jim hadn't worked on it before, and I tried to look at it as he would. So I was distancing myself from that night as best I could."

He sighed. "By the time we arrived Don had been taken to the hospital, but from what the witnesses told us I doubted he would survive. Five bullets in his body at close range? One into his head—we never told the press about that one—but he was still able to speak to the cop on the scene. I've been there when other officers have been killed. But this was especially vicious. Blood was everywhere. While we were collecting evidence, we got word Martin had died at the hospital."

Augusta stroked the back of his neck. "Oh, my love."

"We managed to do our job. But I don't know that I've ever had a feeling quite like that. I was tied in knots inside from anger and grief. I wanted to yell and smash things. But of course, I couldn't. I had work to do."

His voice shook. "When we got back to Detective Headquarters, everyone already knew. The faces I saw..." he stopped for a moment. "It hit everybody hard, like a shock wave had gone through the unit. You know, Don was a war hero, or at least a hero to who knows how many wounded soldiers—a combat medic. He fought in three major campaigns in some of the coldest weather known to man...running out and taking care of the wounded under fire, knowing damned well the enemy could care less about the white cross on his helmet. He survives all that and comes home to die on *our* streets. One of us."

He took a deep breath. "People talk about 'the thin blue line.' You know, it *is* a brotherhood. We look out for each other. And if we don't, who will? Oh, I don't mean we're perfect. Everybody makes mistakes, some more than others, and there are bad apples. But name me another profession where each member of the team gets up and straps on a gun, picks up a badge, and goes out willing to put their life on the line to do everything they can for the citizens they're sworn to protect and serve."

"There isn't one."

"No, there sure isn't. And if one member of the team isn't prepared to do that, they end up off the force one way or another. At least that's the case in this city, under Chief Schrotel's leadership. Don Martin, though…he was one of the best."

Malcolm stared into the distance, as if he were envisioning the crime. "And for one of our own to be murdered in cold blood the way Don was, and then not be able to charge the lowlife who shot him five times…well, unless you're a cop you can't understand what that does to us."

His voice shook. "I stood next to Don's casket and vowed I'd bring his killer to justice. And I've failed."

Malcolm ran a hand roughly over his face. "I know…it's been over four years…" he took another deep breath. "But some things…."

Augusta wordlessly gathered him in her arms, pulling his head to her breast. She rocked him like a child, her own tears mixing with his, and eventually he grew quieter.

Fritz whimpered and laid his chin on his master's knee, sitting as close as he could, trying to offer his own comfort. Mal put a hand on his dog's head and relaxed against Augusta.

"I wish I could think of something wise and comforting to say," she whispered.

"You don't need to say anything. There's nothing anyone could say. I'm sure glad you're here, though." He grew quiet for a moment.

"I've been thinking about these two men. Donald Martin and Wesley Vandergriff. Both cut down in the prime of life. So full of promise. Their lives taken…along with everything they were going to be."

"That must be so difficult for you. Knowing the victims can't be brought back, no matter what."

"You're right, it's never really enough. All we can do is honor their memory, and at least most of the time bring the killer to justice and give their families some closure. But as long as this battle continues—the battle between good and evil—some of us will continue to fight on the side of good. Fight with everything we have."

Augusta kissed him. "My valiant warrior. Keep up the good fight, Malcolm. Every day, you make a difference."

Malcolm touched her face softly as he gazed into her eyes. "You're quite a warrior yourself, bride."

"Warrior bride…I like that," she murmured. "We're quite a formidable team, are we not, groom?"

"Yes, we are."

Epilogue

Christmas Eve, December 24
7:45 a.m.

Augusta was grateful for the warmth of her fur-lined, high-heeled boots as she stood on the frozen ground of Spring Grove Cemetery. The wintry sun peeked over the horizon, and a cold breeze lifted as she drew an edge of her scarf over her nose and mouth, a singer's gesture to help ward off the effects of winter weather.

She and Malcolm were the only people present other than Peter Reichenbach's family. Peter had offered a few words in memory of the man he now accepted as his father, and Pete Junior, dark-haired, tall and handsome, stepped forward and placed a wreath of white roses on the grave. He stepped back to stand beside his younger sister, Emily, and the small group watched for a few moments as the bronze casket bearing the remains of Wesley Vandergriff began its slow descent into the grave.

Peter took the few steps to where Augusta and Malcolm were standing. "Thank you for coming." He smiled as he spoke, and Augusta saw peace in his eyes. "It means a great deal."

"Thank you for including us," Malcolm responded.

Mary Ellen joined them. "The other wreath is for Alice's grave. We're walking over there now. I appreciate your getting up so early to be here."

"Peter, are you home for good?" Augusta asked.

"No, I go back to the clinic on the twenty-sixth, but I expect to be discharged by the middle of next month." He put an arm around his wife's shoulders. "But I'm not going back to the classroom until next fall. I want to spend time with my family and maybe do a little traveling. And I plan to come up with a more reasonable schedule."

"Do you have family plans for the holiday?" Mary Ellen asked.

"Yes, we do," Augusta replied, smiling. "My uncle Len flew in from Pennsylvania yesterday, and our sons and their ladies will be with us for a buffet tonight at our house. And a few close friends will join us."

"That sounds lovely." Mary Ellen and Peter turned to join their children after the two couples exchanged holiday greetings.

As they returned to their car, Augusta commented, "It seems Peter has done what Thomas asked. He's forgiven Wesley and Alice. He seems at peace, don't you think?"

"He does."

She glanced around at their surroundings, snow adorning an already beautiful scene. "It's so lovely here. It doesn't feel like a place of death, you know?" She sang softly, "Thou art for the moment, a portal soon passed; But life is eternal, greater than thou."

"From *Savitri*, the Holst opera, isn't it?"

Augusta stared at him. "I can't believe you recognized it."

"Oh, I'm full of surprises, bride." He grinned as he wrapped a strong arm around her waist and hugged her. "I know you're happy about having a family Christmas. And I loved what you said to Mary Ellen—'*our* sons.' I've never heard you say that. You've always referred to Ryan and Danny as 'my sons.'"

"Well—they are our sons. All of you have convinced me of that." She chuckled. "Thank you for making me a mother, groom."

Augusta stopped stock-still and gaped at him. "Wait. Does this mean I've become an old married lady?"

Malcolm laughed. "You're definitely a married lady. Now and forever. Old? You don't have time for that. You're far too busy getting into trouble."

"I never do it on purpose," she replied, placing a gloved hand on the back of his waist as they resumed their walk. "It just happens. Besides, I had nothing to do with this one. That was your dog's doing, remember?"

"Oh, so he's my dog now?"

"Okay, *our* dog. Wonder what Fritz will dig up next?"

"Don't ask," Malcolm laughed.

Patrolman Donald Martin

Lieutenant Stephen R. Kramer (Retired), Historian
Greater Cincinnati Police Museum

While this is a novel, Cincinnati Patrolman Donald Martin did exist, and men like the fictional Detective Malcolm Mitchell still exist today. They are born into families of grandparents, parents, siblings, and cousins, grow through childhood, adolescence, and into adulthood, and after surviving every challenge, settle into a perception of a future with which they are hopefully satisfied. Then they risk it all to serve their country and/or community.

Don was the fifth of seven children born to Perry County, Kentucky, farmers Claude and Alafair Martin, just after a twelve-year ravaging of the state by Prohibition and the Great Depression. Finding work and raising a family was hard for Claude and he moved his family often. Don's first memories were probably of Grant County where Claude found work as a laborer. Later, the family moved to Ohio—probably either Hamilton or Middletown.

At 17, Don joined the United States Army. Though World War II was over, the U.S. Military was heavily involved in occupations and conflicts all over the world. Then, on June 25, 1950, tens of thousands of North Korean soldiers poured over their southern border and attacked South Korea. America responded and Private Martin, a combat medic with the 8th Cavalry Regiment, 1st Cavalry Division landed at Pohang Dong on July 18, 1950. Most survived the next 549 days and three major campaigns involving intense fighting and vicious weather. Almost 4000 of the Division lost their lives; but untold numbers did not because Don, sometimes braving heavy fire, dressed their wounds and sent them off to MASH units. His uncommon valor was common during the campaigns. Exactly two years after the war began, Corporal Martin was honorably discharged with a Combat Medical Badge, Chryssoun Aristion Andreias (Bravery Gold Medal of Greece) streamer, and a Korea Presidential Unit Citation.

Don returned to Ohio and learned drafting at the Ohio Mechanics Institute. He met Alethea Gail Langley and in 1954 they married. She had graduated from Woodward High School and joined the Cincinnati Police Division as a Junior Typist during June 1953. A year later she was promoted to Clerk Typist II and landed the prestigious position as secretary to the second most powerful man in the Police Division, Lieutenant Colonel Henry J. Sandman, Chief of Detectives.

It is likely that Sandman heard of Don Martin's military experience and recruited him. Don was appointed to the 30th Recruit Class during April 1956. He began his career rotating from District 4 (Hartwell), to District 1 (West End), to District 7 (Walnut Hills), three of city's four most violent districts. He handled these assignments with ease. Each of his commanders commented about his effort toward continuous improvement and his affability. Four years into his career, he earned a performance evaluation of 90%, extraordinary for a new patrolman.

Five years into their marriage, Don and Gail applied to become adoptive parents. Early in 1961 they were notified that a baby was available from the Protestant Orphan Home. On February 12, 1961, Gail resigned in anticipation of finally becoming a mother. The family would need an automobile.

On March 10, 1961, Patrolman Martin beginning his shift at 11 p.m., received his sergeant's permission to check out the used car lot at 715 Reading Road when the calls for service died down. At 3 a.m., he notified Police Communications that he would be on foot in the area. He parked his patrol car across the street from the car lot.

When he was forty or so yards from his car and police radio, Don saw two men stealing a battery from one of the cars on the lot. He approached them and a violent struggle ensued, during which his coat was ripped, several buttons were pulled off, and one man gained control of his revolver and shot him in the chest. Unarmed and probably already mortally wounded, Don turned and ran. The man shot him twice more in the back. He slumped to the ground, held his hands up, and the man took deliberate aim and fired another round into his back. The officer fell to the ground and the man walked up and fired a fifth shot into his head behind his left ear.

Another man, sitting in a getaway car, saw the shooting and drove away. The man fired the final round from the revolver at the fleeing vehicle. The gunman than ran up an embankment, tripped and fell using the revolver to stop his fall and plugging the barrel into the ground, and ran up Dandridge Alley and discarded his bloodied shirt into a garbage can. His brother ran in the opposite direction back down toward Thirteenth Street.

Passersby saw the last moments of the drama, drove to a phone booth, and called Police Communications.

No one knows the thoughts that Don had during the next few interminable minutes as he heard silence, then sirens, then someone approach. Did he think of Gail? His mom? The child he would never see? The boys he could not save in Korea who had wounds like he now suffering? When Sergeant Max Abel came to his aid, Don said, "I've had it." Those were his final words.

Nor can anyone imagine Gail's devastation. She just left her job of six years, lost her husband, and, without a husband, lost her baby. Don's parents, siblings, nephews, and nieces lost their son, brother, and probably favorite uncle.

Every police officer, whether they knew Don or not, felt a terrific loss. The thin blue line is a tight-knit group and every death is a loss. But a murdered officer is an abomination, especially one who had survived hazardous duty in war only to come home and be gunned down on the city's streets. A quarter of the officers had never experienced a murdered cop. More than half had experienced only one, and that was six years before.

The other detectives—all of whom were called in that morning—worked around the clock for days to solve the murder of the husband of their boss's popular secretary who just resigned to care for a new baby that she would never see. But there were no suspects nor evidence, other than a shirt discarded in a trash can.

Gail Martin, without a job, a child, or a husband, returned to her position with the Police Division on March 20, 1961. She met Thomas Fegan at the coffee shop at City Hall and they married during August 1962. A year later they moved to Michigan and raised a family. She would be 70 before knowing who killed her first love. His parents and some siblings would go to their graves without ever knowing.

More than a year after the murder, Personal Crimes Squad Detective Jerry Schimph received word from an informant that 29-year-old Walter Walls had, while in prison for the third time, bragged about killing the officer. During 1958, he had been sentenced to the Ohio State Penitentiary for altering car titles. He was paroled in 1959 and sent back again during January 1960 as a parole violator. On February 23, 1961, he was paroled again. He was in Cincinnati when Patrolman Martin was killed. Three months later, he was caught carrying a firearm and sent back to prison.

On August 3, 1963, Detectives Schimph and Stagenhorst traveled to the penitentiary with the shirt, and it fit Walls, but he admitted nothing other than having bragged about the murder. He claimed that was false bravado.

Walls's family and friends, if they knew anything, would not talk. Walls had abused them mercilessly and they knew that he had already caught up with his "getaway" driver and killed him. In 1969, he convinced his girlfriend to kill his estranged wife and the girlfriend went to prison. The only other witness was his accomplice and brother, Jesse Walls. The detectives tried again during October 1963, but Walter Walls would not budge. The case was filed as a cold case in about 1966, but detectives occasionally revisited it during the next few decades.

Then, during February 2005, a tipster called Crime Stoppers with information. The Crime Stoppers investigators brought it to the attention of their boss, Major Offenders Unit Commander (and this author) Lieutenant Stephen Kramer who took it to the Homicide Unit Commander, Lieutenant Michael Zwick. Lieutenant Zwick assigned two Homicide Unit investigators, Kurt Ballman and Jeff Schare, neither of whom had been born yet when Patrolman Martin was slain.

Walter Walls had died six months earlier. Jesse Walls was also dead. The investigators talked to Walter's son and daughter who were, for the first time in their lives, not in mortal fear of telling the story. They related what they had heard over the years from their father and uncle. More important, they claimed that he told them that he put the last shot into Patrolman Martin behind his left ear—a detail that had never been disclosed and that only the killer would know. The Homicide Unit and Hamilton

County Prosecutor closed the case by "death of the offender", Walter Walls.

Three years later, Gail (Martin) Fegan, 73, died on July 13, 2008.

Artifacts from the case are on display at the Greater Cincinnati Police Museum.

Acknowledgments

It was surprising to learn that very little literature came from the 1918 pandemic, the so-called "Spanish flu." Even more surprising was learning that, at least in this country, those who lived through the pandemic managed to develop a kind of cultural amnesia about it.

Last March, reading John M. Barry's fascinating and frightening book, *The Great Influenza* (written in 2005), helped me understand the lack of literary works during that period. Once it was over, people wanted to forget it. Will we just want to forget COVID-19 when it's over? I find I am unable to write about the current pandemic as our country struggles through this terrible time.

Still, the similarities between the two pandemics are striking, and since my mystery series is set in the twentieth century nearly fifty years after the Spanish Flu—and fifty plus years before COVID-19—I was intrigued to find a way to incorporate what I'd learned about the earlier pandemic in my latest novel.

As for the plot—I recently said to a friend, all stories begin with *what if*:

What if a murder was committed in October 1918 in Cincinnati? *What if* the killer had a way to hide that body in such a way it would be securely concealed? *What if* nearly fifty years later, quite by accident, the remains of the victim were unearthed?

And *what if* Homicide Detective Malcom Mitchell had been assigned to attempt one last time to close a recent cold case, and as he was working on this, he was also assigned the case of that decades-old murder? When I approached Lt. Stephen R. Kramer, my partner in crime (so to speak) for each of the Augusta McKee mysteries to ask if he was aware of the Cincinnati Police Department having dealt with such a case, I truly struck gold. Yes, there was such a case, the murder of a young patrolman, Donald Martin, in 1961. And most amazingly, that case wasn't closed until more than forty years later.

For this book, Steve generously shared with me his file on the Martin case, and also agreed to write an addendum to the book about the case and its final resolution. Historian for the Greater Cincinnati Police Historical Association and Museum, Steve himself had a long and distinguished career with the CPD, an organization at one time considered the finest law enforcement agency in the country while under the exemplary leadership of Chief Stanley Schrotel, a name which has appeared in several books in the series. My heartfelt thanks for Steve's support, assistance, and encouragement on this journey.

Ashleigh Evans has become much more than my editor. She has come to know Augusta and Malcolm as well as I do, and she corrects, suggests, and provides thoughts that become part of the story. In the early stages, we exchange ideas, and eventually come up with the bones of a plot (pun intended) which grows into the finished product you now hold in your hands. I know how fortunate I am to enjoy this collaborative effort.

Taylor van Kooten has once again provided an excellent cover which captures the elements included in the story. I especially like this one, with the watch as its center, since the story covers two periods in time: 1918 and 1965. Taylor is a gifted artist and designer, and I thank her for the striking images which are the first impression the reader has of Augusta's world.

Many thanks to fellow author and friend John Abel, who put me in touch with the Monroe County Historical Association which provided information about the 1918 pandemic here in Northeastern Pennsylvania.

Thanks to fellow musician and friend Gary Raish who provided some assistance with my 1918 obituaries and other items relating to the funeral director business. Local people may see something of Gary in my character Gary Ridgeway.

I am grateful to my generous and supportive Beta readers, who were willing to read the book in manuscript form and let me know if it actually was a book. I appreciate their enthusiasm for this sixth installment in Augusta's mysteries and for the series: Michaele Benedict, Audrey Duffield Henry, Marti Lantz, Eric Mark, Susan Prtune, Nathaniel Taylor, and Ken Van Camp.

And as always, my thanks to friends and fellow writers in the Lady Writers of the Poconos who read parts of the book and provided valuable input: Sahar Abdulaziz, Belinda Gordon, Kelly Jensen, Evelyn Infante, Mary Anne Moore, and Catherine Schratt.

I enjoyed bringing Augusta and Malcolm to the Poconos for a visit in this book, something I've wanted to do for a long time. Now that they've been here, is it possible they might be back? Mysteries seem to be drawn to Augusta wherever she might be!

Susan Moore Jordan
Pocono Mountains
Fall, 2020

Videography

Savitri Chamber Opera by Gustav Holst
        Janet Baker, Robert Tear, *soloists*
        English Chamber Orchestra,
        Imogen Holst, *conductor*

Danse Macabre by Camille Saint-Saëns
        transcribed for organ
        Gert van Hoef, *organist*

Isle of the Dead by Sergei Rachmaninoff
        Royal Concertgebouw Orchestra
        Vladimir Ashkenazy, *conductor*

Floods of Spring by Sergei Rachmaninoff
        Transcribed for piano and performed by
        Ji Liu

"Prelude and "Liebestod"
        from *Tristan und Isolde* by Richard Wagner
        Boston Symphony Orchestra
        Leonard Bernstein, *conductor*

Requiem by Gabriel Fauré
        Judith Blegen, James Morris, *soloists*
        Atlanta Symphony Orchestra and Chorus
        Robert Shaw, *conductor*

The Lark Ascending
        by Ralph Vaughan Williams
        Hilary Hahn, *violin*
        London Symphony Orchestra
        Sir Colin Davis, *conductor*

MAN WITH NO YESTERDAYS

'A thoughtful, superbly paced historical novel
looking at the emotional damage of war.
A FINALIST and highly recommended.'
The Wishing Shelf Book Awards. 2019

CHAPTER 1

I was born somewhere over the South China Sea on a medical transport plane en route from Vietnam to Walter Reed Hospital by way of Japan. Or it might be more accurate to say I was re-born, because at the age of twenty-two those became my earliest memories for a long time.

The first thing I remember — hearing the hum. It sounded far away, but it grew louder, filling my ears and my head. *My head.* It felt strange; heavy and achy. I was lying on a bed or a cot of some kind. A sudden lurch, then a sharp drop. Then a leveling off. The humming grew louder again, then quieted. *A plane. I must be on a plane.*

I became aware of terrible pain in my left leg. *Broken? Something's wrong with it.* I must have groaned, because somebody next to me said, "Captain? I think he's awake."

I forced my eyes open and there, hovering over me, a face staring into mine. My head was throbbing. I had trouble focusing; he looked blurry. "Glad to see you back with us, Sergeant."

"Unh."

"Don't try to move."

I groaned again.

"We're taking you home. Enjoy the ride."

None of this made the slightest bit of sense. The plane lurched again and my stomach went with it.

"Home?" I kind of croaked it out. My mouth felt like crap … cottony. A spoonful of ice chips placed on my tongue made me shiver. But the cold wetness tasted good.

"We're almost to Japan. We'll land briefly and some patients will be de-planed. Then we're flying to the U.S. To Walter Reed Hospital."

A military hospital? What the hell am I doing in a military transport plane?

The guy … I figured he must be a doctor … who had been talking to me, gently opened my eyes and shone a light into them. My head ready to explode, I tried pushing his hands away, but other hands pulled mine back down.

"Sorry, Sergeant. I know this is uncomfortable. I need to check to see how your pupils are reacting to light. You've had a severe concussion and you probably feel confused right now."

You got that right, genius. He switched off the light. "Are you in pain, Sergeant?"

"Yes … my head. And my leg."

"Your leg was broken in the crash. We're giving you pain medication. Try to rest easy for the remainder of the flight."

I felt a prickling on the back of my hand. Opened my eyes again and saw an IV attached to that hand. Closed my eyes; they didn't feel right.

I was hurting and I was scared. *I don't know what the hell is going on. Sergeant. Was that what they had called me?* I drifted off.

As the plane took off I woke up again. The huge, deafening roar hit me hard, and then I felt the plane lift. I made myself open my eyes; a guy in uniform stood close by. *What's that word again? Medic, I think. Yeah, medic.*

"Medic?"

He moved closer. "Yes, Sergeant? How ya doin'?"

"Do you have …" I tried to find the words, they were swimming around in my head somewhere. "That … those … ice chips?"

He gave me a stingy half spoonful. "Easy, Sergeant. Just a little at a time." He adjusted the IV. "Leg feeling any better?"

"Yes, it's … okay."

"Try to rest."

"The … the Captain? He said I was …" I had to stop. It hurt to think and I couldn't come up with the words I needed. I tried again. "In … in an … in a … crash?"

I guess this must have been above his pay grade, because he said immediately, "I'll get Captain Turner."

I tried to focus. But my eyes still hurt and the back of my head felt heavy.

The Captain reappeared and he looked the same. *One thing I can hold onto. Nothing else makes any sense.*

"What can I do for you, Sergeant?"

"What happened? I can't … remember … anything."

"There's time enough to discuss this later. You need to rest for now."

"No! Tell me."

The Captain chose his words carefully. "You were in an accident. You received a blow to your head when you were thrown from the helicopter you were in. We're transporting you to Walter Reed Hospital for treatment."

Most of this didn't make any sense at all, but I hung onto one thought. *My head was hit. Or I hit my head.* My leg throbbed. "What about … my leg?"

"It's been put in a cast. You never had a broken limb before?"

Fear is strange. It wraps around your insides like icy tentacles and starts pulling all the blood out of you. Leaves you cold everywhere. I started to shake.

"I don't know. I can't remember."

I must have looked like shit, because he seemed concerned. "That's normal, Sergeant. When you get that bad a whack on the head, it makes it hard to think. Is your leg still hurting you?"

"Captain … Turner, right?" He nodded. The fear thing inside me started to grow bigger and bigger. "I don't remember … anything. *Anything.*"

He placed a reassuring hand on my shoulder. "Easy, soldier. Do you know where you were before you woke up in this plane?"

"No. Wait — Vietnam? There's a war …" I did know that. And the uniforms I could tell were Army. So I must be in the Army.

"Yes. You're Sergeant Jake Cameron, Special Forces."

The fear thing backed off a little. I had a name. That helped. Captain Turner must have figured I meant it when I said I didn't remember anything.

I could breathe a little better. "Thank you." I tried to focus, and came up with something. "Is it 1970?"

He grinned at me. "January, 1971. Good for you."

"And Richard Nixon is president, right?"

"See, Jake? You do remember some things."

"My eyes hurt. And my leg is … is killing me."

Captain Turner reached up and did something to the IV.

"Go back to sleep, Sergeant. When you wake up we'll be home."

***

After a lifetime as a musician—performer, teacher, musical theater director—Susan Moore Jordan wrote and published her first novel in 2013 at the age of seventy-five, and she hasn't stopped since.

In her first four novels, the author drew from her life experiences as a voice teacher and stage director, and those historical novels were inspired by real people she encountered.

"Companion" novels, *Memories of Jake* and *Man with No Yesterdays* were released in March and November of 2017. A departure from her earlier historical novels, these two books detail the struggles of two brothers, Andrew and Jake Cameron, whose lives were irrevocably changed by their service in the Vietnam War. *Memories of Jake* was the recipient of an honorable mention Red Ribbon Award from the 2017 Wishing Shelf Book Awards. *Man with No Yesterdays* was a Finalist in the 2019 Wishing Shelf Book Awards, and Semi-Finalist in the 2020 Kindle Book Awards.

Recently, Jordan has embarked on a "cozy mystery" series, "The Augusta McKee Mysteries." Book one, *The Case of the Slain Soprano*, was released in April, 2018 and *The Case of the Disappearing Director* followed in October, 2018. *The Case of the Toxic Tenor* was next in April of 2019, and book #4, *The Case of the Purloined Professor* in September, 2019. Books #5 and #6, *The Case of the Chrysanthemum Murders* and *The Case of the Unearthed Evidence*, were released in May and October, 2020. *The Case of the Slain Soprano* was a finalist in the 2018 Wishing Shelf Book Awards and a semi-finalist for the 2020 Kindle Book Awards. *The*

Case of the Disappearing Director was a finalist in the 2019 Wishing Shelf Book Awards.

All of Jordan's books are "music-centric" (in the words of one reviewer), and readers comment on the strength of the element of music included in her work. Jordan sees writing as another way to share the music she loves, which she considers "the most powerful force in the universe."

Articles by Susan Moore Jordan have appeared in *Musical America* and *The Guardian*, and on August 2, 2019, she appeared on Hour Three of "The Today Show" as a Super Senior.

***

If you enjoyed
The Case of the Unearthed Evidence,
please consider leaving a reader review
on Amazon. Reviews are a standing
ovation! They are also valuable to indie
authors and greatly appreciated.

Links to all my books can be found on
www.susanmoorejordan.com

www.ingramcontent.com/pod-product-compliance
Lightning Source LLC
Chambersburg PA
CBHW070556260626
47161CB00002B/622